Where in the world is nobility found without conceit?
Where is friendship without envy?
Where is beauty without vanity?

Here one finds gracefulness coupled with power,
And strength tempered by gentleness.
A constant servant, yet no slave.
A fighter, ever without hostility.

Our history was written on his back.
We are his heirs.
But he is his own heritage;
The horse.

The noble ones accept the yoke.
They serve, but never will be slaves,
For to themselves
They never can be traitors.

Hans-Heinrich Isenbart,
'The Kingdom of the Horse'

Dancer

Shelley Peterson

The Porcupine's Quill

CANADIAN CATALOGUING IN PUBLICATION DATA

Peterson, Shelley, 1952-
Dancer

ISBN 0-88984-177-2

I. Title.

PS8581.E8417D36 1996 JC813'.54 C96-931755-7
PZ7.P48Da 1996

Published by The Porcupine's Quill, 68 Main Street, Erin, Ontario NOB 1TO. Readied for the press by John Metcalf. Copy edited by Doris Cowan. Typeset in Ehrhardt, printed on Zephyr Antique laid, and bound at The Porcupine's Quill Inc.

Cover is after a photograph of Jennifer Foster riding Zeus at the Barcelona Olympic Games, courtesy of Karl Leck/USESA. Interior pen and ink sketches by Marybeth Drake.

Represented in Canada by the Literary Press Group. Trade orders are available from General Distribution Services.

We acknowledge the support of the Canada Council for the Arts for our publishing programme. The support of the Ontario Arts Council and the Department of Canadian Heritage through the Book and Periodical Industry Development programme is also gratefully acknowledged.

For Ben; for Adam;
and for Chloë, who was the inspiration for 'Mousie'

Contents

Chapter One

The Royal

THIS WAS IT. The Royal Winter Fair. Tension electrified the air. It was even scarier than Mousie had imagined, and she'd been having anxiety dreams for a week. She took a deep breath and carefully positioned her reins. Dancer quivered in anticipation. Mousie reached down to pat his sleek neck. The elegant chestnut stallion pawed the ground and nickered quietly to her, giving her courage. She mustn't, she couldn't look into the stands where her mother sat. One glance at that hopeful, loving face and Mousie knew she'd crumble into a useless heap. She was thankful that she couldn't see any faces at all through the glare of the floodlights. Mousie thought she was going to pass out.

'Get a grip,' she scolded herself through clenched teeth.

The starting whistle blew. She steeled herself. She nodded to the judge and whispered into a silky, delicately pointed ear, 'Time to get the job done, Dancer.'

'Number ninety-seven. Daring Dancer. Owned and ridden by Hilary James.' Mousie hardly heard the announcement as she and Dancer started their gentle canter into the first jump. There were so many noises from so many directions that Mousie's ears muffled everything into an indistinguishable hum. It was just the two of them alone in the enormous ring.

'Easy does it, Dancer.' Dancer set himself properly on his haunches and sprang forward. 'Yes, that's it.' They cleared the imposing oxer with inches to spare and sailed on to the next. Dancer arched his neck and held his tail proudly while Mousie judged his position and faced the next hurdle squarely. Over they went in perfect harmony, horse and rider completely synchronized.

Way up in the stands, hardly daring to breathe, sat Christine James, Mousie's mother. In her early forties, she was still attractive in her slim, refined way. She wore tan pants and brown paddock boots, with a cream turtle-neck sweater and tweed jacket, her fine dark shoulder-length hair swept off her classic features. Even though her clothes were well past their prime, they were of good quality and worn with style.

Christine watched her sixteen-year-old daughter and the young horse with wonder. Tall and lithe, pretty and bright, Mousie was a beautiful sight on her powerful mount.

Who would've believed it, she thought. Absolutely no one. Just about two years ago, with no money to spend, they'd bought this creature. He was a rebel horse. Mangy and mad, that's what they'd said about him. No one could get near him to look after his feet, and he kicked and bit. No wonder they could afford him. And look at him now. A hair's breadth from becoming a winner at the Royal Winter Fair, Canada's greatest horse show. Mousie's patience and kindness, consistent hard work and an uncanny communication with Dancer had turned him around. Christine looked in awe at her child.

Hilary had been nicknamed Mousie by her father, and the name had stuck. Auburn-haired and passionate, he'd been very close to his only child. They were soul-mates, aligned in spirit and sharing the same sense of fun. Mousie had been devastated by his death two years earlier. Peter James had been a wonderful man and a loving father. He'd been larger than life, a compassionate and generous person with a booming laugh that matched his humorous temperament.

The cancer that claimed him had also taken the light out of his daughter's eyes. Mousie had gone into a serious depression, avoiding friends and dropping all her interests. She didn't have any energy, and her teachers complained that she fell asleep at school. Her health was failing, too, because she had no interest in food. Christine had been at her wits' end trying to help her overcome her grief, until the day that crazy horse had come into their lives.

And into their lives he'd come. At a full gallop! Christine and Mousie had been out in the barn doing the chores when pounding hooves echoed louder and louder until coming to a dead stop in front of the barn. They'd run out to see what was happening. There he'd stood, head proud and unrepentant with nostrils flaring from his escape from his owner, who'd been leading him down the road to a prospective buyer. The two of them had stared at this chestnut vision, and it was then, Christine reflected, that the light had returned to Mousie's eyes.

The farmer had been overly eager to sell, and the price was suspiciously low, but Christine had asked no questions. People had warned her against buying him, and the vet was truly alarmed. But Christine knew what she was doing. Her daughter needed this horse. Heaven knew Christine didn't. It was hard enough making ends meet without the expenses of a seventeen-hand, underfed, ill-mannered, pig-headed, wormy stallion.

Christine's eyes continued to follow her daughter's brilliant ride around this very difficult course. She marvelled again at what love can do. There was no question in her mind that the strong bond between horse and rider was creating this magic.

There was another pair of eyes watching the ring. Samuel Owens, considered by many to be the foremost authority on horseflesh in Canada, whistled softly under his breath. Yes. This was the real thing, he thought. Perfect conformation. Deep chest, great muscled hindquarters, flat knees, straight legs, limber movement, alert eye, marvellous bearing. Likes what he does, sane, attentive manner, good judgement.

Samuel Owens cracked his knuckles and started tapping

his foot. Must have that horse. Olympic material. Perfect for my niece Sara.

Mousie looked ahead. A triple combination – three big jumps in a row. Steady in, and over clear. And stride, set up straight, and over clear. And steady, set and over clear. Done. Right lead, focus set, and stride and stride and stride and stride and over the four-foot stone wall with a huge aggressive-looking black-and-white plastic cow standing right beside it.

'Good boy, Dancer. You ignored that nasty thing. I know how you hate cows. We're almost home.' Mousie always talked to her horse and she didn't care what anybody said about it.

One fence to clear and the class was theirs. There had not been one clear round yet, and Mousie and Dancer were the last to show in this final jump-off.

They rounded the last turn. The crowd was with them. Mousie stretched Dancer's stride subtly to get his pacing perfect. She balanced him onto his haunches. Like liquid gold they flowed over that last five-foot jump, clearing it by a fraction of an inch, and the cavernous arena came alive with yells and hoots and wild applause.

They exited the ring, Mousie acknowledging the cheers with a smile and a nod, Dancer with a triumphant kick.

Christine found herself standing, tears of joy streaming down her face. Her beloved Mousie had won the coveted Fuller Trophy.

Dancer and Mousie were called back first into the ring. Christine watched as the lights dimmed and the spotlight shone on Dancer, prancing proudly into the centre. Mousie was smiling broadly, and the crowd was applauding with great enthusiasm. Then, as the sixty-five hundred people filling the Coliseum watched, Dancer drew himself up onto his hind legs, and stood for five full seconds. There was not a sound to be heard. Just when it seemed that he could balance no longer, he lightly dropped his front legs down and made as grand a bow as could possibly be imagined, with his nose touching the ground. The whole place erupted in chaos. This was a moment that no one there would ever forget.

The heat of their euphoria settled into a lovely glow, as mother and daughter drove the old truck home later that night, pulling their patched-up horse-trailer behind them. The familiar shapes of the gracious, rolling hills of Caledon pleased their eyes and soothed their spirits after all the day's excitement.

'Tell me again Mom, was Dancer wonderful?'

'He was magnificent. Strong, handsome, and glossy, and he took every jump without hesitation. And remember, you had the only clear round in the jump-off. There wasn't a horse there that even came close.'

'Mom, do you think it's possible that people watch from Heaven? I mean after they're dead?'

Christine considered the question. 'Are you thinking of your dad, Mousie?'

'Yes. It sounds so weird to say out loud, but I swear he was with me the whole time. It was Dancer and me and,' Mousie paused and shook her head, 'I swear Dad, too. Do you think I'm going crazy?'

'No, honey. I'm sure you're not. Things happen sometimes that can't be explained. And you loved your dad very much, and I'm sure you wished that he was there tonight.'

'So you think I imagined that he was?'

'Maybe.'

'But maybe he really was there?'

'I can't answer that. I wish I knew.'

'Well, I know he was.' Mousie sat for a few minutes in silence.

'One thing I know for sure, honey,' Christine said, 'is that he'd be very proud of you. You were fabulous. Totally in control, guiding him just enough. Nobody rode with the skill and sensitivity that you did. You looked beautiful. Talented and confident. I'm very proud, too.'

Mousie hugged herself, beaming with pleasure, as they turned off Heart Lake Road onto the Olde Base Line. A few kilometres west, they made a right onto a gravel road that wound around a tree-covered hill. Hogscroft, their century-old home, was on the right just as the road straightened. It'd been called 'Hogscroft' since it was first built, named for the business that the first farmer ran. He had raised pigs, and lovingly called the place after his treasured animals.

They made the turn up their drive very carefully, as the rains had washed out some of the culvert by the edge of the road, and drove slowly up past the house to the barn. By the light of the moon they could see on their left the outline of their cosy, dormered stone cottage covered with vines that flowered in summer. Christine believed that a little gardening could hide a multitude of sins. Unfortunately, she thought, it couldn't repair the roof, and that was a worry with winter almost upon them. She didn't want to start thinking of that now. Or about paying the taxes or university for Mousie. It was too happy a night to let her financial worries get her down. Lots of time for that.

Mousie looked at the same sight and sighed with perfect contentment. She loved their little house, with its odd nooks and uneven floors. Every creak in the floor had a special memory for her. She wouldn't trade it for a palace. And she wouldn't trade Dancer, either. She was the luckiest person in the world to have a friend like him. She felt she could burst with happiness.

They pulled up to the stone bank barn, built into the hill over a hundred and fifty years before, and Mousie jumped out as they rolled to a stop.

'Dancer, we're home.' she called and she opened the side door of the trailer. Christine lowered the ramp and guided

Dancer's hind end down the creaking ramp as Mousie gently held the rope at his head.

They walked into the barn and took off the handsome blue-and-white checked blanket they'd received that night along with the trophy. Christine and Mousie chatted happily as they rubbed him down and babied him, before bedding him down in his freshly cleaned stall for the night. They listened for a few minutes as Dancer crunched his oats, slurped his water and munched his hay, feeling that all was right in the world.

Samuel Owens was not happy. Not happy at all. Chad Smith, his trainer, was an idiot. Owens had given him a dressing down. He'd deserved it. What kind of game was he playing? Spend all that money on the best horses and the best training, and get beat out by a kid? A girl with nothing. A no-name horse. A no-name stable.

What really made his blood boil was that he'd once had the chance to buy him and had turned it down. The horse had looked untrainable and crazy to him, and he'd ordered the farmer off his property. What had he been thinking? How could he have guessed the potential of this animal? Chad should've known. That's what he paid him for. He'd tell Chad tomorrow that he was finished. This was embarrassing. Even humiliating.

Owens paced back and forth in his mahogany-panelled den on his Persian rug, dropping ashes from his Havana cigar. He had the best of everything. He always said that otherwise it wasn't worth having. And now, goddammit! he didn't have the best horse. Must have that horse. For Sara to ride in the Olympics. A lifelong dream. An Owens winning gold. His only sister's only daughter. He could see it now. Sara on the podium reaching out for the gold medal, stopping to wave to her Uncle Sammy, everyone cheering. He stopped dreaming abruptly. He needed that horse.

Hold on, hold on, this should be easy, he thought. Everything has a price.

I won't fire Chad tomorrow, he mused. Chad can pay these James people a little visit, and feel them out. Figure out what will buy this horse. He didn't want to be seen himself. Prices shot sky-high when people knew you could pay. Yes. That's what he'd do.

Samuel Owens pulled on his suspenders with his thumbs, grabbed his cigar with his teeth bared, and grinned. He felt considerably happier.

Chad had no trouble finding Hogscroft from the directions given at the Coffee Bean Cafe on Highway 10, where he'd picked up another pack of Player's. Luck would have it that they were almost neighbours. It was a clear and vibrant fall day, the kind that makes you glad you're alive. Chad was also glad to be employed. He reminded himself that he wasn't getting any younger, and remembered what the boss had said. This was his chance to redeem himself. No horse, no job. And jobs were not that easy to get. Not with his little drunk-driving record. And a few other small run-ins with the law. Especially jobs like his, with good horses to work with. Chad knew horses. He also liked the prestige of working for one of Canada's top stables. It put him a good notch or two above the crowd.

Samuel Owens was a good boss, he thought. You don't cross him, though. Too often he'd seen what happens when you cross him. You better get out of town, quite literally, and start somewhere fresh in a new place. Owens was happy as long as you did your job and followed his orders and agreed with him on everything. No, thought Chad, you don't ever want to cross him. He shuddered with the recollection of what had happened to Roddy, the stable boy. Chad had been the one to find him. Twenty stitches to his face alone. He'd thought he was dead. When Roddy recovered, months later, he'd silently moved to Kentucky, and had wisely kept his mouth shut.

Chad turned up the lane, getting a wheel caught in the croded culvert. He cursed as he backed up his blue Ford sedan, then gunned it up the drive. He passed the house and stopped at the barn. It seemed that no one was home. Just as well. He'd take a look around.

Funny, he thought, no dogs. He stubbed out his cigarette, opened the car door and started to get out.

Racing from the barn were three white, long-necked, hissing geese, coming right for him. He got the door closed just as a billy goat butted the side of the car. Geez! Won't make that mistake again, he thought.

Chad was wondering what to do, whether to wait or come back later, when he heard the frantic barking of a dog. He looked around and saw a brunette getting out of a wreck of a truck. A little brown-and-white Jack Russell terrier jumped right over some bags of groceries in its hurry to defend its mistress and territory.

He was in no hurry to get out of his car. He wasn't looking forward to getting pecked by vicious geese or rammed by a bad-tempered goat or bitten by a rabid dog.

Christine knocked on the window, and he rolled it down.

'Is there anything I can do for you?'

Chad tried a smile. 'You can call off your menagerie.'

Christine assured him that he'd be fine, now that she was there. Chad cautiously stepped out of the car and looked around.

'My name's Chad Smith. I presume you're Mrs James?'

'Yes, that's right.'

'I was at the Royal last night when your daughter won the cup. Most impressive. She's a real horsewoman, Mrs James.'

'Well, thank you Mr Smith. I think so, too.'

'And the horse isn't half bad. Do you mind if I take a look at the him?'

'Dancer? He's right behind you.'

Chad spun around. The magnificent chestnut had appeared from thin air.

'Where'd he come from?'

'From wherever he was. He won't stay in the field, he jumps out. He won't be locked up, he kicks down his stall. So he grazes when he feels like it, comes into the barn when he feels like it, and generally does what he likes.'

'I've never heard of such a thing.'

Christine tilted her head, assessing this stranger. 'Neither had we, I assure you. Dancer is not an average horse in any way.'

'I can see that.' Chad's eyes travelled admiringly along Dancer's elegant lines. He reached out a hand to catch his halter, but Dancer stepped one step back. Chad tried again, and Dancer stepped back again. Christine laughed.

'Okay, you do it!' Chad was known for his skill with horses, and now his pride was hurt.

'I wasn't laughing at you, Mr Smith. It was just . . . funny.'

'Can't you control this animal?'

'We do just fine, Mr Smith.' Christine didn't like his tone. 'May I ask why you're here?'

'Well . . .' Chad wasn't sure how to begin. 'Your horse was admired last night . . .'

'I'm sure he was. He's a stand-out in anyone's books.'

'I'm looking for a horse, and I'm prepared to put in an offer.'

'I'm sorry to disappoint you, but we have no interest in selling Dancer.'

'They say everything's for sale.'

Christine looked at the man long and hard. Chad began to feel awkward. Dancer rested his head on Christine's shoulder and shook his head, nickering gently.

'Mr Smith, they are wrong, whoever they are. This horse is not for sale.'

'Mrs James, I'm sure that we can come to an understanding.'

'What exactly do you mean?'

'I mean I'm sure that I can offer you a price that would make you very happy.'

'This horse is not for sale. There is no offer that could make me happy, Mr Smith. How can I be more clear?'

'You must be a very rich woman to be able to say that.' Chad looked around the modest farm with a sarcastic grin.

Maybe it was his manner, or maybe it was the anger that Christine was feeling towards him. Whatever it was, the animals didn't like it. The geese advanced on him slowly, hissing. Charlie, the goat, lowered his horns. Pepper, the Jack Russell, growled. And Dancer pawed the ground and snorted.

Chad could take no more. 'Perhaps I should call at a more convenient time.'

He jumped in his car and flew down the lane, leaving his tail-pipe in the culvert. Christine heard his loud cursing, and began to laugh. That's the end of Chad Smith, she thought, still chuckling as she carried in the groceries.

'You don't believe me, Mr Owens, but I tell you, the place is spooky. If I believed in witchcraft, I'd say that woman was a witch. The animals seem to be under her spell.' Chad was sweating nervously, switching his weight from one foot to the other, standing at his boss's desk in his den.

'Chad, I don't give a damn about the woman. Is this horse for sale or not?' Owens calmly gazed at the original antique oil paintings of horses on the wall, swivelling on his luxurious red leather desk chair. He appeared bored.

'I'd have to say it's not.'

Owens swivelled to a stop, staring blankly at Chad. 'Not. Not? Is this a joke, Chad? The horse is not for sale? My, my. You say they obviously could use some money, and then you tell me the horse is not for sale? My God, man, everything's for sale.' His mouth was smiling but his eyes were deadly serious.

'Not to these people. Look, this horse maybe isn't what you want anyway. We didn't buy him in the first place because he was so wild. He won't stay in a stall or a field and he. . . .'

Owens cut him off, dismissively and impatiently. 'Don't tell me what I do or do not want. And a horse will do what we make him do. Don't try that on me, Chad.'

'But . . .'

'Chad, I'll say it again.' Owens now spoke very quietly, still smiling. 'Either you get me that horse, or you're fired. With no recommendation.'

'Mr Owens, . . .'

'If you refuse this last chance, then you might as well pack your bags now. And ask yourself how many people would hire you, once they know all the details of your past.' With that, Samuel Owens stood up, signalling the end of the conversation.

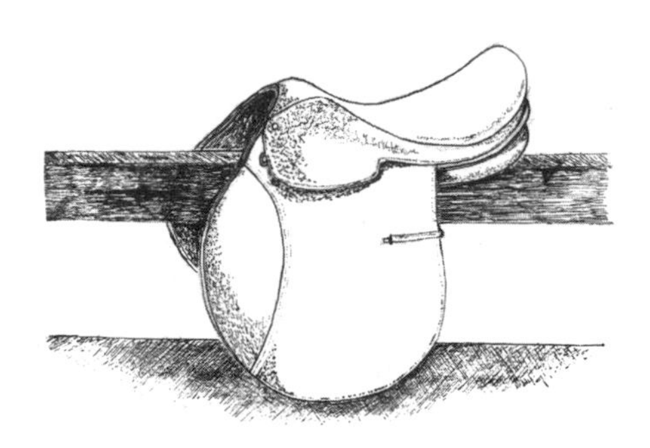

Chapter 2

The Queen's Exhibition

A BEAUTIFULLY ENGRAVED letter, addressed to Miss Hilary James, arrived at Hogscroft. Christine had picked up the mail from the mailbox at the end of their lane in the morning on her way to work. She was to show a young family yet another house. She was tempted to open it, but with a great deal of effort overcame her curiosity. She forgot about it while she did her job as real estate agent, but noticed it again on the front seat of her car as she was driving home. The paper was thick and creamy white. The calligraphy had been done in exquisite script. But most surprising of all, it had the royal seal. It puzzled Christine no end. Who could it possibly be from? Certainly not the Queen!

She tried to put it out of her mind while she went about her day, but she found herself watching the clock for the time when Mousie would come home from school. Mousie wouldn't be home too soon, because she liked to ride her bike as long into the fall as possible to avoid the kids on the school bus.

Later in the day, Mousie slowly pushed her bike up the lane to Hogscroft. She was preoccupied, her head down, and her face sad. School had finished at three-thirty, and it had taken her half an hour to ride home, knapsack on her back and stinky gym clothes to wash in her carrier.

Why were people so mean? she wondered. Why does Sara Preston get such joy from running me down? What's she got against me? I'm always nice to her, even at horse shows where she's so snobby just because she rides with her Uncle's fancy stable with all their grooms and amazing horses and I'm only with Mom. And why do the other girls believe what she says, and avoid me like they do? They call me the 'Country Mouse'. Am I such a joke? What have clothes got to do with a person's value, anyway? Maybe I should buy a fashion magazine and dress more ... like what? We don't have the money, anyway. And I wouldn't want to look like Sara Preston, that's for sure, no matter how she shows off and dumps on me for being a hick. Or that nasty Carol-Ann, Sara's side-kick. And what business is it of theirs that I don't have a boyfriend? Or a date for the school dance. I'd rather be alone the rest of my life than go out with any one of those guys ... well, maybe I'd go to the formal with Sandy Casey. He's cute. And he's nice, too. If he asked me. Which he won't. Anyway, Sara Preston thinks he's going to ask her. Well, they can all go jump in the lake. All those kids. I've got something nobody else has. I've got Dancer. She permitted herself a small smile, but was preparing to plummet back into her gloom.

Christine had been listening impatiently for the sound of Mousie riding up the lane. Finally, Pepper started barking her welcome-home bark. She ran out of the house with the letter.

'Mousie! There's a letter for you!'

'What's so special?' She wasn't quite ready to leave her heavy thoughts, but her curiosity was pricked by her Mother's excitement.

'Open it. It's driving me crazy. Look at the stationery. Who's it from?'

'Mom, you need more fun in your life.' She propped her bike up on the side of the house and took the letter from Christine. 'Holy. Now I see what you mean. This paper's heavy.'

'Mousie, just open the letter.'

'Okay, okay, Mom.' Standing outside, beside her mother, she carefully tore the envelope open.

They read it together, in growing disbelief.

Dear Miss James:

As Head of Organization for the Royal Visit, I am responsible for inviting young Canadian riders to participate in an exhibition to be presented to Queen Elizabeth II. You, as the winner of the Fuller Trophy, automatically have a place, as was publicized.

You may be aware that Her Majesty and Prince Philip will be arriving in Canada on November the 23rd of this year. They will make a tour of the Maritimes, Quebec and Eastern Ontario, then arrive in Toronto on the 28th. That evening, we have scheduled a horse-show in accordance with Her Majesty's wishes.

It will be held in the Coliseum at Exhibition Place, starting at 8:00 p.m. on November 28th.

I am very pleased to invite you and Daring Dancer to participate. We hope to make this an exciting evening, and your involvement would be a highlight.

Please respond as to your availability as soon as possible, and a detailed schedule will be mailed to you immediately. If you have any questions, do not hesitate to contact me.

Yours truly,
Andrew Chalmers, Brigadier

Mousie looked with amazement at her Mother. She shook her head in disbelief. 'I forgot all about this! All I could think of was the Fuller Cup! That's only a week from now!'

'Look on the bright side. You and Dancer are fit.'

Mousie turned and ran to the barn. 'Dancer, you'll never guess. Dancer, come here!'

Dancer trotted out from behind the barn, his chestnut coat glistening in the muted autumn sun, and met her halfway. He whinnied his greetings and pushed her with his nose.

'I take it that we answer in the affirmative?' Christine asked.

'Mama, we're gonna knock 'em dead!' Mousie joyfully

sprang off the garden bench onto Dancer's back and gave him a big hug.

Mousie and Dancer worked every day that week after school in the practice ring; walk, trot and canter, also called flatwork, for strengthening and conditioning, and jumping for practice. She did flatwork every day, only working over jumps every couple of days. She couldn't risk stressing his forelegs and hocks.

Nothing was too much trouble. The Brigadier had given her all the details of the evening, including the dimensions of the jumps and the layout of the course, since this was not a competition but an exhibition. Mousie had set up the jumps in the ring to match it as closely as possible. She wanted nothing more than for them to put on a good show for the Queen.

As the day neared, Mousie felt sure that they were ready to perform. They were jumping in top form. She got butterflies in her stomach every time she thought about it, but it helped to talk about it with Dancer. If anyone had been watching the long-legged teenager with the pretty face and long, silky light-brown hair, chatting away to her horse as she worked him around the paddock, they would have thought she was bonkers. Mousie chuckled at the thought, but she wouldn't have cared.

The morning of the show arrived. At five-thirty Mousie's alarm rang. She jumped into her barn clothes and ran outside to give Dancer his breakfast. While he gratefully chomped on his sweet-feed mixture, she cleaned the muck out of his stall.

'This is the day, Dancer. We're going to have a ball.' She washed out his water bucket and refilled it with fresh, cold water. Giving him his flakes of hay, she stopped to rub his chin. He stretched his head up in the air so she could give him a really good scratching.

'Not too long this morning, Dancer, I've got your mane to braid.' She climbed on the foot-stool, separated his mane and began to work. It took time, and she wanted to do a first-class job. She'd bathed and clipped him the day before, and Mousie was relieved that he'd kept himself clean overnight. Dancer ate his hay while Mousie braided and brushed and shone him up, chattering away the whole time. When he was fully groomed and ready, Mousie gave him a big smooch on the nose and raced into the house to have a quick shower and be off to school.

Christine grabbed her in time to hand her an egg sandwich for her breakfast and give her cheek a goodbye kiss. 'Have a good day, honey, and ride that bike safely.'

Mousie pedalled gaily along the country roads thinking that the day was just perfect. Fall had stayed late this year, a few brightly coloured leaves still clinging to the trees. The air felt cool and fresh, and the strengthening sun was chasing the morning mist out of the hills.

As she rode along, she mentally reviewed her list of things that had to be done. Dancer was groomed to perfection; his coat healthy and shiny, his mane pulled and braided, his feet newly shod and painted with pine tar. The tack was cleaned and oiled. The saddle pad was washed. Her riding breeches were ready and her lucky stock pin, a treasured gift from her father, was polished. Her blouse and tie were white and starched, her boots polished to a gleam, her hat and coat brushed up. Everything was just so. Yes, she smiled, they were ready for tonight.

School dragged the entire day. She looked at her watch every few minutes, wishing she could magically make the time fly. I'm going to ride Dancer for the Queen, she kept thinking. Tonight. Holy. Tonight! Prickles of excitement ran up and down her body every time she thought about it.

'Earth to Country Mouse.' Mousie jumped. Sara Preston was at her desk, giving out papers. 'Dreaming about fame and glory? Forget it. Just so you know, you're not so hot. It's a matter of having the right horse, that's all. It should be me riding for the Queen tonight. At least I'd give it some class. Break a leg, Mouse, I mean it.' She smiled ever so sweetly and continued on down the aisle. Carol-Ann grinned meanly from the next desk.

Even Sara Preston's taunting and Carol-Ann's eye-rolling didn't faze her. She seemed to be in a pink cloud all by herself. It was difficult for her to concentrate on the teachers' lessons, and for the first time that she could remember, she didn't feel self-conscious eating lunch by herself.

School finally came to an end. Mousie was out the door and on her bike almost before the bell had finished its shrill ring. I'd better hurry, she thought as she pedalled furiously towards home. How could I be any luckier? We're riding for the Queen!

Feeling an overwhelming surge of joyful anticipation, Mousie raced her bike up to the barn and whistled for her friend.

Dancer whinnied back, but with a strange urgency.

Mousie jumped off her bike and ran into the barn.

'Dancer. What's wrong?'

'Do you talk to animals, too?' a voice said.

'Who's that?' Mousie stopped dead. 'And where are you?' She heard Charlie baa-ing in a stall as she looked around the darkened barn. Her eyes were unaccustomed to the darkness of the barn after being in the bright daylight outside.

'Down here. Under this wretched animal's hoof.'

Mousie looked down, and sure enough there was a man pinned under Dancer's freshly shod front-right hoof. Mousie stepped closer. He was middle-aged, with a large nose, smallish eyes, and a thin mouth. His cloth cap lay beside him on the ground.

'Who are you?'

'Let me up.'

Dancer shook his head violently and snorted.

'No. You tell me your name and why you're here and

maybe I'll think about letting you go.' Mousie looked at him sternly.

'Look, it's a misunderstanding. I came to the wrong place. I was hired to pick up a horse at Hogs Hollows. They're expecting me. This horse has been standing on me for an hour and a half. Now if you'll just tell him to release me, I'll get out of here and be on my way.'

'You haven't told me your name and I don't believe your story.'

'His name is Chad Smith and he's lying through his teeth.' Christine appeared in the door of the barn with Pepper, the little dog, leaping and growling at the prone man's face.

'Now, Mrs James. Don't go jumping to conclusions. I just came back to see if you'd changed your mind, when the horse attacked me and pinned me down.'

'You're trespassing. And you just lied to my daughter about your intentions.' Christine was trying to control her anger. 'If I ever see your face again, anywhere near my property, I'll have you arrested.'

She made a gesture to Dancer, waving her hand in an upward sweep, and the horse lifted his foot. Chad grabbed his cap as he scrambled to his feet and took off out the back door of the barn, where he had hidden his horse-trailer and car. They listened as he started the engine and sped down the lane. There was the sound of his new tail-pipe and then the trailer scraping over the culvert.

Mousie buried her face in Dancer's neck, and started to sob.

'He was going to take Dancer, wasn't he Mom?'

'We can't be sure, honey. One thing, though, I won't lock up the geese or Charlie when I'm out any more.'

'And leave Pepper here to guard the place, too.'

'You're right. We'll have to be more watchful. I'll let the police know. And I'll get the neighbours to keep an eye out for him, too. Oh, Mousie, honey, stop crying.' Christine put her arms around her daughter. She rocked her and spoke gently. 'We've got to get going. We should leave for the city in less than an hour.'

Christine left the barn to call the police. Her heart was pounding in her ears. She couldn't let on to Mousie just how disturbed she was.

Mousie picked up a brush and began to groom her beloved animal. She started singing through her tears. 'Rolling, rolling, rolling down the ri-ver.'

'That was one of Dad's favourites. Oh, I miss him so much! No one would try that if Dad was here! You never met him. You came here after he died, but you would have really liked him. He was, well, he was ... anyway I've told you all about him many times. I sure loved him.' Tears started falling down Mousie's face. 'Dancer, don't let them take you away, too. I don't think I could stand it.'

Dancer shook his whole body and ground his teeth. Anyone would think that he'd understood everything she'd said.

They were loaded up and on their way in no time at all. Christine was trying to stay chipper to cheer up her red-eyed daughter as they drove toward Toronto.

'You were totally organized, honey. Everything was ready. I'm really impressed.'

'Mom, what if that man had kidnapped Dancer? Where would he have taken him? What was he going to do with him? This has really given me the creeps.'

'Mousie, you saw what Dancer did to him. He knocked him over, pinned him down, and held him for an hour and a half. The man must have been frightened out of his wits. I don't think he'll try anything now. But you make a good point. Maybe we should find out a little bit about him, in case we need to know.'

'You mean in case Dancer disappears?'

'Well, yes. We should know more about this man, anyway.

He's trespassed twice, and that makes me nervous. I'll see if I can find out where he lives and what he does.'

'Good. Then we can creep around his house and spook him out.'

Christine and Mousie had a great deal of fun thinking of ways to scare Chad Smith, and by the time they drove into the grounds of Exhibition Place they were in high spirits. As they passed the main doors of the Coliseum, on their way around to the back where they were to unload Dancer, they slowed to avoid two jaywalking pedestrians.

'Isn't that Rory Casey and his son?' Christine asked.

Mousie felt a blush heating up her face. 'Sandy Casey is here? What for?' She watched them walking in their tuxedos towards the building.

'Judging from the way they're dressed, they must have been invited to the show.' Christine noticed, as she always did, how attractive Rory was. He walked with an athletic, confident stride. His dark hair had silvered and his face was more rugged, but he'd retained his youthful bearing and quick sense of humour. His son seemed to be growing up in the image of his father. Sandy was fair like his mother, but seeing them walking shoulder to shoulder it was abundantly clear that they were father and son.

'Oh, God, Mom! I can't do this if Sandy's here. What if I screw up? He'll think I'm a loser. What if he tells all the kids at school?'

'Is he that horrible a person?'

'Mom, Sandy's a great guy.' Mousie was indignant.

'Then he'll understand if you screw up. And he wouldn't think badly of you. And he most certainly wouldn't tell all the kids at school. If he did, then he wouldn't be worth worrying about. Honey, what's the problem?'

Mousie seemed stricken with nerves. 'I ... well ... I ... care what he thinks. I can't do this. I just can't!'

Christine thought for a moment, considering the impact of

her daughter's current social problems at school. 'Mousie, when you go in that ring, do you go in alone?'

'No. I'm there with Dancer.'

'Exactly. And does he know what he's doing?'

'He's probably only the best horse in the world.' She sounded sarcastic, as if to say her mother should already know that.

'Precisely. So the Queen would probably enjoy watching him jump.'

'Mom, you know she would.'

'Well then, if you can't do it, should we get someone else to ride him tonight?'

'Mom. He only lets me on his back. He'd throw anyone else right off!'

'So. What's your pleasure? We turn around because Sandy's here and deprive the Queen of the greatest thrill of the night, or grit your teeth and get the job done.'

Mousie considered for only a second. 'Let's get this horse unloaded and give 'em hell.'

Once again, only a short time after the Royal Winter Fair, Christine found herself up in the stands of the Coliseum, fondly known for years as the Horse Palace. She'd helped Mousie get Dancer all tacked up, and had left them with the other nervous participants in the warm-up ring. Christine had gone to the stands reserved for the family and helpers of the riders. Beside her sat mothers and fathers and sisters and brothers and cousins and friends. Below her she noticed the hundreds of glittery, well-groomed people sitting expectantly, waiting for the Queen and her entourage to enter.

She examined the backs of their heads until she spotted Rory Casey and his son Sandy. Very interesting, she thought to herself, that Mousie had a crush on Sandy. No wonder, though. He's a good-looking boy and from what she could tell, very nice. But the irony of her daughter falling for the son of her first boyfriend made Christine smile. That was so long ago, before she'd met, fallen madly in love with, and married, Peter. Rory and she had gone through school together and had always been very close, sharing every secret. She'd always thought in the back of her mind that they'd end up getting married. Rory had thought so, too, and it was the only sad note in her story-book romance with Peter. But life had gone on, and Rory had married Helena Sandford-Jones, a beautiful and talented dancer. They'd had two children, Sandy, short for Sandford, and a girl, Rosalyn. Rory had made a success of his father's Hereford farm, and owned the local radio station. He also had an interest in various other businesses and properties. Christine felt happy that his life had turned out so well. She didn't know Helena well, but each time they'd met, Christine had marvelled at her petite, perfectly chiselled features and her lithe gracefulness.

She wondered idly why Helena wasn't at this event. Perhaps there had been only two tickets offered, and Sandy had wanted to come to watch his classmate ride.

Christine felt a familiar sadness tug at her gut. Mousie hated going to school lately because all the kids had started finding her 'uncool'. Christine couldn't figure it out. Mousie had just got on her feet from the pain of losing her father, when the leader of the trendiest girls had viciously turned against her. The other girls didn't dare cross this girl, Sara Preston, for fear that they, too, would be ostracized. Christine sighed. This was a big worry, and she had no idea what to do. Pour on the love, she told herself. Stay off her back about small things, and it'll all hopefully work itself out. Meanwhile, though, Christine had no doubt of the toll this was taking on her daughter's confidence. Mousie didn't speak up in class for fear of being ridiculed. She didn't join teams or go to dances for the same reason. If I ever get my hands on that Sara Preston! thought Christine savagely.

Christine was startled out of her reverie by trumpets

blaring the arrival of the Queen. The audience rose to their feet and all necks craned, trying to catch a glimpse of the royal party. She felt the fluttering of butterflies in her stomach, and imagined how much worse Mousie must be feeling. The Queen, followed closely by Prince Philip, surrounded by bodyguards, made her stately way to the royal box. Now and then she paused to wave to the crowd. Only when she'd settled comfortably onto the cushioned chair could the rest of the crowd be seated.

The big overhead lights dimmed. The spotlight found a tall, slim, elderly man in the centre of the ring, elegantly wearing full evening dress and holding a microphone.

'Your Majesty, Prince Philip, honoured guests, ladies and gentlemen. My name is Brigadier Andrew Chalmers and I am delighted to be your host for a most unusual evening. The royal family's well-known interest in horses sparked the inspiration for a display of Canada's best young riders, performing in their various equestrian sports. At the outset let me sincerely thank each participant, some of whom travelled great distances to bring us their talent. At Her Majesty's pleasure, we will begin. I hope you all enjoy the show!'

He was far more charming than Christine would have thought from reading his stiff invitation to Mousie. She began to relax, looking forward to the entertainment.

The spotlight followed the Brigadier out of the ring, and the lights went up on a Hereford calf racing into the centre, with a boy of about sixteen riding a sturdy grey appaloosa at full speed, in hot pursuit. The crowd was delighted. Around the ring they galloped, the boy now leaning forward, circling a lasso over his head. Faster than Christine could figure out what had happened, the boy had roped the calf, was off his horse, and was tying the calf's feet together. He stood up proudly, took a slight bow, and then untied the calf, to thunderous applause. The spectators had a chuckle at the calf, who had no intention of leaving this appreciative audience until the boy came back out, roped him again, and dragged him away, loudly protesting.

'Thank you, Thomas O'Riley and Aramis from Okotoks, Alberta. Thomas is this year's junior roping champion of the Calgary Stampede and quite the horseman. And Aramis was named "Appaloosa of the Year." '

Men in fringed suede cowboy outfits ran out rolling barrels. They set up for a barrel course in double-quick time, and were barely out of the ring when two girls on matching black-and-white pintos thundered in, weaving in and out of the barrels in synchronized time. It was a beautiful sight, the girls wearing outfits of pure white leather with silver studs, and the pintos sporting red tack. This exhibit was done to 'high-steppin'' western music. The song changed to 'hurtin'' music as the horses moved away from the barrels and slowed into a lope. The girls, who appeared to be in their late teens, started to stand up carefully on top of their saddles. The crowd held its breath as they reached full height, balancing as they continued in a circle around the ring. Then suddenly, at exactly the same second, the two of them hopped back into their saddles and waved at the crowd, smiling broadly.

'That was Nora and Clara Weselowski from Winnipegosis, Manitoba. Thank you, ladies! Junior barrel racing champions of Canada, giving us some genuine western style.'

Christine looked around and saw the proud family hugging each other, and thought that her mother, Joy Featherstone, would've loved to have come. Mousie had been too nervous to want anyone else to come, and her Mother was in Milan anyway. But Mousie deserved a bigger cheering section.

The barrels were cleared away as quickly as they'd been set up, just as two glossy jet-black hackneys pranced in, pulling a buggy driven by a young man dressed all in black. They were stunning as they trotted around, picking their feet up proudly in perfect time. The crowd was treated to a view from all sides as he drove his horses in figure eights. Christine considered the amount of time it would have taken to clean all that black leather. As he drove out, he made a special bow to the Queen, and Christine saw the Queen wave a tight little wave.

'M. Jean LeFèvre from St. John, New Brunswick, and his matching hackney ponies. Youth driving champion of Canada. C'est merveilleux. Merci beaucoup, Jean!'

Beethoven's 'Moonlight Sonata' played loudly from overhead. An immaculately groomed bay Hanoverian glided smoothly into centre ring, front legs extending at a trot. The discipline and refinement of this sport captured the audience's interest. They watched in awe as the pretty young blonde woman took her mount through various difficult manoeuvres, keeping time gracefully with the music. They sidestepped across the ring and danced on the spot, and cantered on different leads every step, making the horse appear to be skipping. Christine felt lucky to be in the crowd, it was such a pleasure to watch.

'Thank you, Katrina Reinhardt, all the way across this fair country of ours, from Victoria, British Columbia. Dressage champion of the year and every inch a showperson!'

Twelve snorting Arabian horses, all silvery grey, with each rider dressed in a different bright colour, galloped clockwise around the enclosure. They sped past in a blaze of glory, stunning the senses. They all came to a grinding halt, reared up as one, and reeled around in the opposite direction, taking off at full tilt. Just as Christine was feeling giddy watching them go round and round, they halted, lined up facing the royal box, and bowed, the horses and riders together. The onlookers applauded joyfully as the teenagers stormed out, as flashy as when they'd stormed in.

'That was the Arabian Society of Merryfield, Saskatchewan, ladies and gentlemen. Many thanks to you all for showing us this spectacle. What a talented group of young people!'

Christine started feeling nervous for Mousie, as each act came and went. She wondered if she could sneak down to give her some moral support without causing alarm among the Queen's security.

There was a Welsh pony ridden over tiny hurdles by a little seven-year-old champion from Nova Scotia that was heart-warming, a thrilling polo demonstration from Quebec, an aristocratic Tennessee walking horse from Prince Edward Island, and a gleaming, enormous team of Clydesdales from Newfoundland. Each act got a marvellous reception. The evening was a success beyond any doubt, and Christine felt proud that Canada was giving the Queen such a show.

Now the tractors pulling the flat-beds of jumps for Mousie motored into the ring. Christine's hands got clammy and she had a strong feeling that Mousie needed her. She wanted desperately to go to her daughter's side. But they had all been told that they could not get up until the royal party had left. Christine swallowed her anxiety and absently-mindedly shredded the programme to pieces.

There she was. Mousie. Christine's heart pounded. Dancer trotted in, loose-limbed and supple. He looked incredible; he appeared to have his own halo of light. The horse carried Mousie with such care! Not for the first time did Christine marvel at the love between horse and rider. The Queen sat forward. Her attention was caught.

As Mousie had been instructed, they cantered to the middle facing the Queen, and bowed her head. Dancer, to the amazement of everyone but Mousie and Christine, bowed as well. This was just one of his many tricks, but a good one nonetheless. Mousie shot a tiny glance to where she imagined her mother to be sitting, then looked quickly away, very nervous but in control.

Dancer collected himself magnificently and cantered into a circle. They were about to start and suddenly Christine felt too nervous to watch. Almost against her will her eyes stayed glued to her daughter and the horse. She said a little prayer that all would go well.

They sailed over the first jump, a big brush. It looked almost four feet high. They took the first triple bar with poetic grace and went on to the six-foot-wide water jump. No problem there.

The Queen was sitting noticeably forward. Now she was gripping the rail in front of her. Mousie and Dancer took the five-foot wall with six inches to spare, and the power of the horse and the skill of the rider made the crowd gasp in unison. The multi-tiered in-and-out was next. This was a frightening-looking thing, Christine thought, a big jump constructed of red and white horizontal poles, with room for the horse to take just one stride before leaping another identical jump.

The horse and rider glided toward the in-and-out, Dancer eager and cool, Mousie fearless and steady. Dancer took off at exactly the right spot and soared into the air.

Then it happened. Mousie, with the saddle flying, shot up over both jumps and came crashing down onto the dirt floor of the arena. She made an effort to get up, then flopped. She didn't move.

Christine shoved the stunned spectators unceremoniously out of her way, scrambling down the tiers of seats toward her daughter.

Dancer jumped the second of the two jumps by himself and came to a stop beside Mousie. He nuzzled her. She lay still. Red Cross people raced to the scene, but Dancer wouldn't let anyone near. He lashed out and bit one man and turned to kick another. Nobody was going to get close. There were cries of 'sedate the horse', and 'she's broken her neck'. Pandemonium had broken loose.

Christine yelled, 'Let me through! I'm her mother!' but she couldn't get close to the field. She screamed again, 'Mousie! Mousie!' but no one heard. Just as Christine was about to panic, strong arms grabbed her, pushed her through the crowd, and lifted her over the barricade. She landed in the ring and ran full out to Mousie.

'Get that lady off the field!' a woman shrilled.

'That lady is the girl's mother! Let her go!' yelled a very familiar voice. Christine couldn't think about who it belonged to then, she needed to get to Mousie.

Dancer whinnied his deep, powerful whinny when he saw Christine. He nudged her gently with his nose and let her past to kneel over Mousie. But he kept everyone else back. There were two other people keeping the crowd at bay; Rory and Sandy Casey. It had been Rory, Christine now realized, who'd lifted her over the barricade.

Mousie was knocked cold. Christine thought that her arm was broken, but not anything else. Probably not her neck, but one should take no chances. Mousie stirred a little.

'You'll be fine, my darling girl. Everything's going to be all right.' Dancer put his nose to Mousie's face and sniffed. Christine rubbed his nose and said through the lump in her throat, 'Dancer, we'll have to let them take her.'

Christine held Dancer's head gently while the ambulance men warily passed the now tranquil horse and put Mousie on a stretcher. Christine wondered what to do with Dancer. She desperately wanted to go with her daughter, and time was of the essence. Dancer whinnied to Mousie as she was carried out.

'She'll be all right. You'll see. People aren't all bad, Dancer, although it seems that you think so. Now, I just have to figure out how to get you home.' As she was talking to Dancer, Rory came up to them.

'Christine, let me take the horse back to Hogscroft for you.'

'Rory, you're the answer to my prayers. I'll jump in the ambulance with Mousie.' She started to hand Rory the reins. 'Our trailer is just behind the ...'

Before she could finish her sentence, Dancer reared up, whinnying loudly. Rory tried to reach for his head to help hold him, but Dancer spun around away from him, shaking him off. Christine spun with him and pulled him around, tears of frustration stinging in her eyes. 'Rory, it won't work. He won't go with anyone he doesn't know, and the ambulance can't wait for me to load him for you.'

Rory considered the situation for a brief moment and waved across the chaos to his son. 'Sandy! Go!'

He turned back to Christine. 'He offered to go to the hospital with her anyway. He'll follow in a cab if they won't let him ride with her.'

'Thanks, Rory. That makes me feel better. A whole lot better.'

'Let me help you with the horse.'

'That's okay, Rory. It's probably better if you don't. But thanks. I'll get him home and then come back down to the hospital.'

'Let me follow you home and you can leave the truck and trailer there. I'll drive you to the hospital in my car.'

'No, I'm really fine.'

'Christine, let me help. You think you're fine, but it's still a shock. I'm following you home whether you like it or not. Have you forgotten how stubborn I am?'

'Thanks, Rory, that would be great.' Christine smiled her thanks and led Dancer toward the exit. She remembered the saddle. She turned to go back for it, but she saw that Rory had it slung over his arm. He really was a good friend. She avoided all the well-wishers and headed out to the trailer with Dancer.

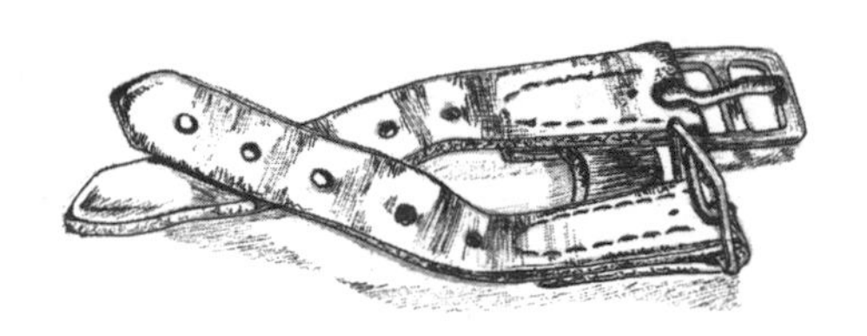

Chapter 3

The Caseys

CHRISTINE HAD NO trouble loading Dancer into the trailer and getting out of Exhibition Place. She could see Rory in her side view mirror, and was grateful that he was there. Although she hadn't seen him in a few years, it seemed as if their friendship was undiminished.

All she could think about was her daughter, unconscious, in the hospital. At least Mousie wasn't alone. How had that accident happened? she wondered. How could the saddle get loose like that? Christine had tightened it herself. And Mousie always checked the girth before she went on. This was troubling. She'd take a look at the saddle when she got home. Christine tried not to think at all until she got to Hogscroft.

They pulled up to the barn and she unloaded Dancer, who seemed strangely subdued. Whoever claimed that horses were stupid had never met Dancer, she thought.

As Christine was quickly feeding and watering the animals, Rory came into the barn, carrying the saddle with a pensive face.

'Rory, let me look at that. Something must have snapped for the saddle to come off like that.'

'It didn't snap, Christine. Look at this.' He showed her the elastic at the end of the girth, which holds the saddle onto the horse. It had obviously been cut, leaving only an eighth of an inch on either side of it to bear the weight of the rider over all those big jumps. It would have held for a short time, but there would not have been any chance of its lasting for the entire round.

'Oh, Rory. That's been cut. It looks like scissors or a knife.'

'Who would have done that?'

Christine looked at Rory and paused. 'Let's talk in the car. It'll take the better part of an hour to get to Sick Kids.'

Rory drove quickly but safely toward the hospital. Christine sat in the passenger seat, intent on getting to her daughter and relieved that she wasn't driving. Her hands were shaking.

'Okay, Christine, let's talk. Do you have any idea of who might wish Mousie harm?'

'How would anyone get access to the girth? When I left her and went up to the stands, Dancer was tacked up and Mousie was warming him up.'

'Maybe she had someone hold him for a minute.'

'Dancer doesn't stand still for just anyone, Rory. He goes crazy. You saw that tonight.'

'Well, someone got to the girth with scissors after you'd left. I'll start asking questions tomorrow.'

'Rory, have you ever heard of a man named Chad Smith?'

'No. Why?'

Christine took a deep breath and started to tell the story of the man who'd trespassed and possibly tried to steal Dancer. When she told him about Dancer holding him down in the barn, Rory couldn't help but laugh.

'If I didn't know Dancer, I wouldn't believe it!'

'How do you know Dancer?'

'His previous owner, Terry Behrens, tried to sell him to my wife. Helena loved his looks, but she couldn't get near him. She insisted on riding him, so Terry tied him up and hoisted Helena onto his back. She lasted exactly one second.' Rory started to chuckle at the memory. 'Once Dancer was free of her, he chased Terry around the paddock, screaming, until I caught him. It was terribly funny.'

'Funny? Was Helena hurt?'

'Oh, no. Otherwise of course it wouldn't have been funny.

But it showed us all what a character Dancer is. I'll tell you now, Christine, I thought you were totally crazy to buy him.'

Christine laughed, distracted momentarily from thoughts of Mousie. 'I thought so, too, believe me! But he seemed different with us. And we adjusted to his ways, too. He's sure been good for Mousie.'

'The two of them were made for each other. I had goose bumps watching them. I've never seen anything like it. And the Queen was mesmerized.'

They were pulling up to the hospital. 'Rory, thanks for being such a friend.'

'Look, Christine, I want to help. This is sabotage. Or attempted murder. I'm going to find out who this Chad Smith is. He might be responsible.'

After leaving the car in the parking lot, they strode quickly into the hospital, Christine bracing herself for the worst. She led the way to the reception desk.

'I'm Christine James. My daughter, Mousie, or Hilary, was brought here tonight unconscious ...'

'Yes. Here it is.' The receptionist efficiently located the paperwork. 'Mrs James, go on up to room 313. She hasn't regained consciousness yet, and the doctor wants to talk to you.' She turned to Rory. 'And you are Mr James?'

Rory shook his head. 'I'm a friend of the family. My son came in with the ambulance.'

They rode up the elevator and walked down the corridor, Christine numb to the sights and sounds and smells. When they got to the door of Mousie's room, the nurse cautioned them to be quiet. They entered.

Christine looked down at her daughter. She was pale and looked so young and vulnerable. Christine brushed her daughter's face gently with her hand and murmured, 'I love you, honey.'

She appeared to be sleeping. Christine reminded herself that she was in a coma. Sandy had stood when they'd come in, and now he moved up beside Christine.

'Mrs James, she hasn't moved or anything. I hope she's all right.'

'Sandy, you're a great kid. Thanks for staying with her.'

'I wanted to. In case she woke up and didn't know where she was.'

The doctor bustled in. He was middle aged and kindly, but obviously busy. 'Mr and Mrs James? I'm Dr Porter. I have every reason to believe that your daughter will regain consciousness shortly. Her signs are excellent. She has a broken arm, which we'll set when she comes around. She sustained no other injuries in the fall, about which this young man has kindly filled us in. Other than her head injury. If she regains consciousness in the next short while, I believe that she'll most likely be just fine.'

'Most likely, Dr Porter?' Rory spoke up. 'What exactly does that mean?'

'Ah, well, there's always a little mystery in head injuries, Mr James.'

'My name is Rory Casey. This is my son Sandy. We're friends of the family.'

'Ah, yes. Well, I must go, but I'll be back to check on her. Please call the nurse should she come around.' Dr Porter was out the door.

Mousie moved.

Christine took her hand. 'Honey, Mousie, it's Mom, honey. Mousie, my honey.' Mousie opened her eyes.

Mousie looked solemnly around the room, blinking, and then saw her mother. 'Mom. What happened?' Her voice was hardly audible.

Sandy vanished down the hall calling, 'Dr Porter! Dr Porter! She's awake!'

Christine squeezed her daughter's hand and said, 'Mousie,

you had a fall. You have a broken arm and a concussion, but you'll be fine. How do you feel?'

'Not great. Awful, actually. Weird. Where's Dancer? Can I go home?'

'We'll have to see what the doctor says.'

'I want to go home, Mom. What if that man Chad Smith tries to steal Dancer again?'

'Don't worry about anything, Mousie. Rest and get better. I'll look after Dancer.'

'How can you look after Dancer, when you're here?'

Dr Porter and Sandy entered the room. 'Ah yes, that's better! Awake, now, Hilary?' Dr Porter cheerfully shone light into her eyes with his ophthalmoscope, and felt her pulse.

'I'd like to go home now, Doctor.' she said, trying hard to sound healthy and strong.

'Ah well. A little soon for that, Hilary. I'd like to see you tomorrow and make that decision. Better stay here tonight.'

Rory had left the room when the doctor'd entered, and now he was back. 'Mousie, don't worry. I've called Mack Jones the police chief, and he's got someone checking on things.'

Little tears sprang unbidden into the corners of Mousie's eyes. She faced her mother. 'Mom, please, let's go home now.'

Uncertainly, Christine turned to the doctor. 'Dr Porter, would it be all right if I took her home?'

'Mrs James, she must be kept here for the night. Much safer. She's concussed. If she were to slip back into a coma, what would you do? And we have yet to set her arm.'

'Mousie, you'll have to stay,' Christine said, 'and I'll stay with you. The police are watching the farm, and there's nothing to worry about.'

Rory spoke up, having noted the great anxiety that Mousie was feeling about Dancer. 'Sandy and I will spend the night at Hogscroft. We'll come to get you and your mother tomorrow. Would that make you happy?'

'Mr Casey! Sandy! Sorry, I didn't ... I guess I didn't see you. I'm sorry, I ...'

'Mousie, don't worry, you had a bad fall, and you've got lots of things on your mind.' Rory smiled warmly at the pale girl in the hospital bed. 'Come on, Sandy, let's go.'

Sandy stepped up to the bed. 'Hilary, you rode really great tonight. You're the best rider I've seen in my life. And I'm glad you're awake. I was worried.' He smiled. 'No, actually, I was scared.' Mousie feebly smiled, fervently wishing that she didn't blush quite so easily.

'Oh, Rory, the keys.' Christine tossed him her ring of keys. 'Thanks so much. I mean it.' She gave Rory and Sandy a big, grateful smile.

The Caseys left. After Mousie's arm had been encased in a fibreglass cast, Christine sat by her bed holding her hand. They chatted about this and that until Mousie drifted off to sleep. Christine tiptoed out to arrange for a cot to be brought to Mousie's room. The cot arrived within a few minutes, and she promptly fell asleep, deeply grateful that Mousie was going to be fine, and that they had friends like the Caseys.

Sandy and Rory got halfway up the lane at Hogscroft, when they realized that something was terribly wrong. It appeared that the barnyard was strewn with dead animals. In front of them lay a prone Jack Russell. They could see other shapes that were undefined. When they got closer, they could make out a goat and some geese.

'Sandy, you stay in the car. I'm going to check the barn.'

'No, Dad, I'm coming with you. The light's on. Someone might be in there.'

'You're right. But be careful. Stay with me.'

They crept up to the barn and listened. No sound. Rory slowly opened the door, and peeked in. Nobody there. They both walked in. Nothing. Absolutely nothing. No Dancer.

'Dad. Hilary was right to worry. Someone took Dancer.'

They heard a shuffling noise outside the barn. 'Shh.' They hid in a stall to watch. The shuffling noise continued. Then a little thump.

'Dad, I'm going to see what that is.'

'No, Sandy. Wait. It's coming this way.'

They didn't have to wait long. Pepper, the little Jack Russell, struggled in and then thumped down.

Rory and Sandy rushed out of the stall to see if she was all right. 'She was drugged, Sandy. My God, I'll bet they were all drugged.'

'That's the only way they could've got Dancer, Dad.'

'This is serious, son. Come on, we have lots to do.'

They carried the goat and the geese into the barn and onto beds of straw and bundled the little dog into the house. While Sandy tried to revive Pepper, Rory started making calls.

'Chief of police, please ... Mack, it's Rory. I'm at Hogscroft. The animals were drugged and the horse has been stolen. ... Look, can you find out about a guy named Chad Smith? ... No, don't come over. No need.... Christine's at the hospital with Mousie.... No, why tell her now and upset her? There's nothing she can do from the hospital and they need their sleep.... Let's see if we can track him down.... Okay, Mack, I'll wait right here.'

'What's happening, Dad?'

'Mack's trying to find out something about this Chad Smith person. He's our most likely suspect. We're to wait here for Mack's call. He's trying to dig something up.'

'Shouldn't we call Mom?'

Rory looked at his watch. It was midnight. 'She'll still be out with her bridge group, but you're right. I'll leave a message on the machine. Do you want me to get you home? You're still in your tux, you know.'

'So are you, Dad,' he grinned. 'I really want to help. I feel bad for Hilary.'

Rory looked at his son and smiled. He was feeling proud.

Sandy was asleep on the couch with Pepper curled in his lap, and Rory was just nodding off, when the phone rang. They jumped out of their skins.

'Hello!.... Yes, Mack.... Wow. He works for Owens?... Thanks ... He's probably got the horse over there somewhere.... Look, Mack, I know you can't search without a warrant, but I have to try to get the horse back.... Yes, but possession is nine-tenths of the law.... Just do me a favour, give me a little time to try.... I'll call you later.' Rory hung up and said, 'Come on, Sandy, let's go.'

They flung their coats over their crumpled tuxedos, locked the door, and took Pepper with them as an afterthought. They jumped into their car and sped over to Samuel Owens' immaculate estate.

They'd been neighbours for years. Their properties abutted. Unpleasant rumours of violence had swirled around Owens for years, and Rory avoided doing business with him on principle. Certainly he'd never trusted the man, but still he was shocked that he'd blatantly steal a horse.

They turned off the headlights and slowly idled to the barn. It was in total darkness. They got out. Pepper sniffed around.

'Go to work, little friend. Find Dancer.' Rory knew what he was doing by bringing the dog. She sniffed around the barn and over to the yard. She disappeared into the dark, and the men could hear her sniffing more excitedly and then whining.

'Dad, she's on to something. Let's follow her.'

They walked unsteadily in the pitch black, and then Pepper started barking. 'Shh! Pepper!'

They could make out her little white body in the darkness over by a shed. They ran as softly as possible, and tried to open the shed door. It was locked and bolted. Pepper became more excited. Sandy picked her up and petted her, 'Take it easy, we're doing our best.'

The sound of shuffling came from inside followed by a little nicker.

'There's a horse in there that someone doesn't want anybody to find. Any guesses?' Rory talked to Sandy while picking at the lock.

'Dad! Lights just went on at the house! Hurry!'

Rory picked up a big rock and chopped at the lock. It gave.

'Dad, someone's coming.'

Rory quietly opened the door and groped in the dark. Immediately, his hands found the shape of a horse. If this is Dancer, he thought, the poor guy's been doped to the gills.

'Easy, boy. We're here to help.' Remembering how Dancer had pulled away from him at the Royal, Rory took time to convince the horse that he could trust them. 'We're going home, Dancer.'

Dancer nudged Rory's chest with his nose. Relieved, Rory led him out. Pepper jumped out of Sandy's arms and leapt joyfully at the horse's head. The horse groggily nuzzled her and nickered sleepily.

'It's Dancer, Sandy.'

'Dancer's not black, Dad.'

Now that the house lights were on they could see more clearly, and the horse in front of them, indeed, was much darker than the bright chestnut they'd come to find. But Pepper knew him, and he knew Pepper.

'Hey, you! Hey! Who's down there!' A voice bellowed from up near the house.

Father and son made their decision. As he murmured soothing words to Dancer, Rory hoisted Sandy up onto his back, fashioned reins out of baling string tied to his halter, and slapped his rear. 'Get out of here as fast as he'll move.'

Dancer shook his head again and again as he tried to wake up. He wobbled unsteadily toward the gate.

'Sandy, they're closing the gates! Must be automatic. Move it!'

'I'm trying, Dad! He's asleep!'

'Stop! Hey! I've called the cops!' Search lights were now playing in circles around them.

Rory got his car out of the yard and onto the road before the gates could close, and ran back. He grabbed the halter and started to pull while Sandy kicked what he hoped was Dancer, in the ribs. The gates were inching closer together. Rory pulled with all his might. Pepper barked and nipped at his heels. They couldn't do it. The horse was too heavily drugged. Rory stepped out of the driveway just in time. The heavy iron gates clanked shut. He had to think of something.

Now Dancer started waking up. He sniffed the air and sneezed.

'Finally! God bless you, Dancer. Let's motor!' Wide-eyed, Sandy held on for dear life as the powerful animal again shook his head, backed up a few steps, and made a mighty leap over the gate. Sandy could feel himself sliding over Dancer's neck, and he groaned in fear. He thought he was about to smash his head on the pavement and die. With an agile motion, Dancer shifted him back in place and when he was sure that Sandy was fine, took off toward home. Sandy rode unsteadily at first, then he got his balance, squeezed tight with his legs, and wound Dancer's mane through his fingers to get a strong hold. As he gained confidence, he whooped for joy. He was having the time of his life. They cantered, then galloped down the road, Pepper with them every step of the way.

Rory drove behind, praying that it was too late at night for traffic. What have we done? he thought. Other than perhaps stealing a horse. Let's hope it all turns out well.

Rory followed his ecstatic son on the flying stallion up to the barn at Hogscroft, with a huge smile on his face.

'We did it! We did it, Dad! We got him back! Did you see

how fast we went?' Sandy slid off and promptly fell to the ground. His legs just gave out on him. Pepper licked his face, and Sandy laughed.

Dancer settled happily into his stall, grateful to be home. Rory took a good look at him. His coat had been dyed jet black. No doubt it was Dancer, though. No mistaking that fine, intelligent head.

'Mr Owens will have you for horse theft!'

Rory spun around. 'Why, good evening. You must be Chad Smith?'

'That's right. How d'you know my name?'

'Lucky guess. Interesting that you would think to look here for the horse, isn't it? It's almost like you knew the horse would gallop home.'

'That's Mr Owens' new black horse, Spirit.'

'Do you have any proof?'

'Proof! That's ridiculous. You stole it off the Owen property.'

Sandy rushed in on still-wobbly legs, 'Dad, the police are here!'

Chad smiled. 'I called the police when you were stealing the horse. I told them to come here.' Chad was feeling pretty proud of himself. Owens would be pleased with him.

Mack Jones entered with another officer. 'It's two-thirty in the morning. This had better be good.'

Rory and Sandy tried to conceal their relief that it was Mack who'd picked up the alarm. He showed no sign of knowing anything about this. Rory admired his acting.

'These two thieves stole Samuel Owens' new horse, Spirit. I caught them in the act. Arrest them.'

'Let's have a look at him. Lead him out, Smith.' Mack leaned against the wall.

Chad nervously licked his lips. He didn't want to go near

Dancer after his previous experiences, but all eyes were on him. He had no choice.

He went into the stall, and tentatively reached for the halter. Dancer's head snaked out at him, teeth bared. He cornered Chad and lunged.

'Help! Help!'

'You say this horse belongs to Owens?' Mack asked casually.

'Yes! Now get me out!' Dancer turned his back to Chad and gave a mighty kick. There was the sound of screaming mixed with splintering wood.

'Jesus!' Rory jumped to look. Chad was in a dead faint. Dancer had placed his steel-shod hooves just inches on either side of him, missing him but scaring him beyond what he could take.

Mack and Rory looked at each other. 'I swear it almost looked like he meant to miss him!' Mack was amazed.

'And lucky thing, too,' nodded Rory. 'He wouldn't have had a chance.'

'Let's wait a minute before pulling him out,' said Mack, 'He's coming round.'

'Get me out of here!' The yell came from the bottom of the stall. Rory and Sandy stifled a chuckle.

'Chad, is this really Owens' horse?' Mack lazily repeated the question.

'No. Now get me out!'

The officer and Sandy dragged Chad Smith out of the stall. Dancer munched his hay laconically. He did not look like the same horse that had splintered the stall.

'Nice dye job, Chad,' Rory deadpanned, holding up his blackened hands. The dye wasn't even dry.

Chad hissed something unintelligible under his breath.

'I'm taking you in for questioning. Move it!' Mack growled. He signalled to the officer and they watched as Chad was escorted into the back seat of the cruiser.

‘Sandy and I will sleep here, just in case,’ Rory told Mack.

‘No need, I’m sure. But call if you need me. I’ll fill you in tomorrow.’ Mack got in the cruiser and drove down the lane. Rory and Sandy watched them go.

‘Well, Dad, that was quite a night. Now what can we do for fun?’

‘Get in the house!’ Rory playfully punched his shoulder and the two Casey men had a laugh. They checked on the animals, who were recovering well from the drugs. They turned off the lights, and with a great deal of satisfaction, went off to find a place to sleep in the house.

Chapter 4

Love and Confusion

THE NEXT MORNING Christine awoke in her hospital cot feeling rumpled and not quite refreshed. She looked at her watch. It was eight o'clock. She stretched and looked over at Mousie. Mousie was sitting up, already awake and looking pale but perky.

'Good morning, Mom. Let's go home.'

'We have to wait for the doctor. How are you feeling?'

'I'm a little stiff but I feel fine. And my arm won't heal any faster here. There's no reason to stay.'

'Look, Mousie, we can get dressed and ready just in case, but the final decision belongs to Dr Porter.'

Christine assisted dressing Mousie, not an easy task with a tender arm in a sling. They got toothpaste and soap from an orderly, and in a short time they were ready to go. Christine went down the hall and asked the nurse when Dr Porter would be in.

'He's checking on a patient now, and then he'll be in to see Hilary. Oh, just a moment, please.' She answered the phone, and after a brief conversation, she turned to Christine and said, 'That was the doctor. She's fine to go if her eyes are clear. He'll check her now.'

The nurse went down the hall, and Christine used the phone to call Rory to come pick them up.

'Hello?' A raspy voice answered.

'Rory?'

'No, this is Sandy. Is this Mrs James?'

'Yes. Good morning, Sandy. Did I wake you?

'Oh, ah, no!'

'Sleep well?'

'Uh, well, yes! Very well. Can we come pick you up?'

'Thank you, Sandy, that would be terrific.'

'How's Hilary?'

'Feeling fine.'

'Great. See you in an hour.'

'If the traffic moves well. Bye.'

Rory and Sandy groggily struggled awake. They felt like they'd only just gone to bed. They found what they needed; face cloths, toothpaste and such, and since they'd slept in their clothes, they were ready in minutes.

'These tuxes are ready for the garbage. Just look at us!' Rory laughed.

They fed the animals and got in their car. Sandy said, 'Dad, we forgot to call Mom this morning.'

Rory nodded. 'Oops!' He got out, unlocked the house and used the phone.

'Hello?' Her voice was unfriendly and thick.

'Helena. It's Rory. Did you get my message?'

'Yes.'

'We stayed here last night to guard the place, and now we're going to get the Jameses at the hospital.'

'Well, aren't you the hero.'

'Helena, please don't start.'

'Rory, I don't care what you do or where you go. You know that. So why bother calling?'

Rory paused. His head started to hurt. 'I called because our son still thinks that we're a family. He didn't want you to worry.'

'Oh. How nice. Goodbye.'

Rory stood for a moment beside the phone. When had it all gone bad? Was there any hope for them? Were they even the same people that they'd been when they'd fallen in love? All the same old questions flooded his brain. Can't dwell on them now. Put on a happy face and go out to Sandy. Don't involve him in your problems. Think about it later.

Rory got back in the car, turned to his son and said heartily, 'Thanks for reminding me to call. Your mother was worried!'

During the drive into Toronto they talked about their adventures of the previous night, and congratulated themselves on their courage and prowess. They were feeling quite proud of themselves as they pulled into the turn-around entrance at the hospital. Mousie and Christine were waiting outside, Mousie in a wheelchair with a nurse behind. 'Do you think Hilary's kind of pretty, Dad?'

Rory looked at his son, startled. 'Yes, I think she's very good-looking, Sandy. She takes after her mother.'

They all got settled into the car, with Rory and Christine in the front, and Mousie and Sandy in the back.

'So, anything happen at the farm last night?' Christine asked.

There was a little pause, then both men laughed out loud. They laughed until Mousie finally yelled, 'What happened?'

Sandy wiped his eyes and said, 'It's a long story, but it has a happy ending.'

By the time they got to Hogscroft, Christine and Mousie had been brought up to date. They sat open-mouthed, not knowing what to think.

'Holy. To think we slept through the whole thing!' Mousie gasped.

As they turned in the drive, Christine noticed that the red flag on her mailbox was up. 'Do you mind stopping so I can get the mail?' she asked.

'No problem, but it's odd that there's mail. It's Saturday,' said Rory, as he stopped the car.

'It must have been hand dropped,' said Christine as she got the letter and popped back into the car. They drove up the lane.

'Look!' cried Mousie. 'Look at all the flowers at the door!'

Indeed there were. Baskets and bouquets of flowers of all kinds and colours. 'Good grief,' she said. 'Who are they all from?'

Christine had just taken a look at the letter. 'Oh, Mousie.' she spluttered, 'A letter from the Queen!'

'Mom, don't be silly.'

'Mousie, I am dead serious. This is a letter from the Queen of England, herself. Here's the royal seal.' She held up the letter.

Still in the car, Mousie tore open the envelope and read aloud.

Dear Hilary:

Your performance last night was breath-taking. Congratulations. We hope that you are recovering well from your unfortunate fall. We may request that you perform for us again, but next time you might finish the course.

Good luck to you,
Elizabeth R

Everyone was struck dumb.

'A little royal humour, eh Hilary?' noted Sandy. '"Next time, you might finish the course"?'

'Wasn't that a thoughtful thing for her to do,' Christine finally managed to say.

'That's a keeper, Mousie,' smiled Rory.

Just then, a big black horse came walking around the barn. He whinnied in greeting. Mousie and Christine laughed out loud.

'It's a good thing you warned us about Dancer's colour,' said Mousie. 'He looks like a different horse!'

'That was the whole idea,' Rory said, gravely. 'There still are a lot of unanswered questions.'

'If only Dancer could talk.' Mousie walked over to her horse and stroked him lovingly. She rubbed his ears and scratched his chin. They were very happy to see each other, after all that they'd been through.

'Don't you want to see who these flowers are from?' Sandy asked Mousie. They carried in the flowers, and had an enjoyable time reading cards from friends and well-wishers, and admiring flower arrangements.

Dancer grazed outside the window.

Christine had brought in coffee, hot chocolate and toast, of which Pepper successfully weaselled her fair share. A fire was lit in the grate, and there was an aura of well-being in the room that comes with good company. The room was warm and welcoming, decorated with simple good taste over the years. The tall beamed ceilings and multi-paned windows had an old charm unmatched by modern designs. Sandy looked around the room, feeling totally at home. He wondered why he didn't feel this way at his own much grander house.

'This one's from the Brigadier. It's so nice of him,' sighed Mousie.

'Read it,' Sandy said.

'To a very brave and talented Canadian. Thank you for your participation. Get well soon. Andrew Chalmers, Brigadier.'

'My, isn't that nice.' Christine filled the cups and left the room to put on the kettle.

There was a knock on the door. Mousie got up to answer it.

'Sit down, Mousie. Look after your arm,' Christine scolded as she opened the door. Outside stood a boy of about ten. He looked nervous.

'Hello,' said Christine. The boy just looked at her.

'Is there something I can do for you?' she asked. The boy looked over his shoulder, and Christine followed his gaze. A little girl, a year or so younger, was holding his bike, while straddling her own. 'Tell her!' she called.

Christine sized up the situation, and gently insisted that they both come in. Stoically, the little girl lowered the bikes to the ground and approached the house. The boy didn't move until she nudged him, and they came into the house, side by side.

'Please sit down, children. Would you like some hot chocolate?' Christine asked.

'Thank you. That would be nice,' said the girl. 'Patrick, you'd better tell them.'

'First let's get your cocoa,' Christine told them, 'and then we'll hear all about it.'

While her mother was getting cups from the kitchen, Mousie was staring at the boy. 'I know you from somewhere. Where do you live?'

'We live only a mile down the road but you met me last night at the horse show,' he whispered. 'That's what I wanted to talk to you about.'

Rory appraised the boy kindly, as Christine gave them their drinks. 'What's your name?' he asked.

'My name is Patrick Flanders, and this is my sister Molly. She has nothing to do with this, she just wanted to come with me. It's all my fault.'

'I came because you didn't want to tell at first.' Molly piped up.

'I'm telling, aren't I?' retorted her brother.

'Now, kids, it's all right,' Rory said. 'Just what is it that you wanted to tell?'

The little boy gathered his nerve and said, 'I held Dancer last night while you went to the bathroom before the show.'

Mousie exclaimed, 'Yes! That's how I know you! You were there last night, and offered to hold him. Dancer wouldn't have stood still for an adult, but he likes children.' She explained this to Sandy and Rory.

'Our dad was at the Coliseum last night helping some neighbours with the horses, and he let me come if I would help, so that's why I was there.' Here he paused.

'And so, what happened?' Christine coaxed.

'When she,' he pointed to Mousie, 'was in the bathroom, a man came up to me and told me he was her coach. Dancer didn't like him, I think, because he made bad noises at the man and tried to kick him.'

'But you didn't let go?' Mousie asked.

'Oh, he never pulled on the rope.'

'That sweet horse,' said Christine to Rory. 'He wouldn't want to hurt the boy.'

'And the coach wanted to fix something on the saddle. He said there was something sticking out that would hurt Dancer if he didn't cut it off. So he fixed it with a jack-knife. It wasn't easy to do, either, with Dancer jumping around.'

They all looked at each other.

Rory asked him, 'Did you mention this to Mousie when she got back?'

'No. I didn't think it mattered because he was her coach. When the saddle broke, I started to think about it. I told my sister Molly, and she thought the man might be a bad man. Then I remembered how Dancer didn't like him, so I came to tell you. We know you live here because we always see Dancer in the field. If I did something wrong, I feel really sorry. I had bad dreams last night that it was all my fault.' The little boy was sitting, head down, his trembling hands clenched in his lap. He was expecting a scolding.

Mousie knelt beside him, and kindly said, 'Thank you for coming to tell us, Patrick. Now we know what happened. You did me a favour by holding Dancer, and you couldn't possibly have known that the man wasn't my coach. You did nothing wrong, only good things. You held Dancer for me, and now you've come to help solve a mystery.'

Patrick's eyes widened. 'I helped solve a mystery?'

Mousie chuckled, 'You sure did.'

'What did the man look like?' Christine asked.

'He had a cap on and a big nose and he's old. He smelled like cigarettes.'

'Bingo. Chad Smith.' Christine and Mousie looked at each other, and then at the men. 'That's the same man who trespassed and tried to take Dancer.'

'And who stole Dancer last night. It all ties in. I'll call Mack Jones and fill him in,' Rory said. 'And you'll have to make a decision about prosecuting. I can recommend a lawyer, a friend of mine who doesn't overcharge.'

The Flanders children ate cookies and drank more hot chocolate while Rory made his call. They felt happy and warm when they left Hogscroft on their bikes a little later.

Towards noon, Rory and Sandy reluctantly got out of their comfortable armchairs and left Mousie and Christine sorting through flowers and writing thank-you notes. Since Mousie had broken her right arm, Christine wrote what Mousie dictated, then Mousie scrawled her signature with her left hand. It was drizzling and cold, a perfect day for staying inside by the fire.

Christine looked through the window at the lingering reds and yellows and oranges of the leaves, contrasting with the green fields. The colours were misted by the cold rain, but vibrant still. How beautiful this country is, she thought. Ever changing through the different seasons, but always beautiful.

She was startled by the ringing of her telephone.

'Hello?'

'Mrs James?' It was a gruff, low voice.

'Speaking.'

The phone went dead.

'Hello? Hello?' She hung up, troubled.

'What was that all about, Mom?' asked Mousie.

'We must have been cut off. Whoever it was will call back.' Christine wasn't as calm as she tried to let on. The last thing Mousie needed was more anxiety. She tried to think of something constructive they could do to fill the afternoon happily, preferably away from the phone.

'Mousie, how do you think we can get the dye off Dancer's coat?'

'Hmm. I bet a hairdresser would know. Connie's mother's a hairdresser, I'll give her a call.'

They tracked down a gallon of stripping agent at a pharmacy and went to work on Dancer. They were cozy and sheltered in the barn, as the wind and rain slapped at the windows. Mousie sat on the stool with her arm in a sling under her coat, petting Charlie, throwing crumbs to the geese, and playing with Pepper, while Christine worked at Dancer's coat. It was a slow business, and messy, but by dinner time the chestnut was starting to reveal itself under the black.

'It will probably take longer for Dancer's coat to be normal than my arm will take to heal,' Mousie grumbled on their way back to the house.

Dusk had fallen quickly, another sign that winter was coming. It had gotten colder while they were in the barn, and the wind was stronger. They protected their faces from the gusts and hurried on. It was a comfort to them that the animals were all snug on clean bedding and well fed on a night like this.

Mousie and Christine pulled the door behind them and locked it, and hung up their coats. They turned on lights and Christine relit the fire in the main room. Mousie settled herself into a huge armchair, resting her broken arm. She picked up her book and started to read, while Christine checked the kitchen for something to make for dinner. The phone rang. Christine started. Could it be the previous caller? It rang again.

'Hello?' she answered.

'Mrs James?'

'Who is this?' It was the same voice that she'd heard earlier.

'You've been out.'

‘Who is this?’ Christine felt a stab of nerves in her stomach.

‘Chad Smith. Don’t hang up.’

‘You could’ve killed my daughter, cutting through her girth like that.’

‘She’s alive, isn’t she?’

‘She’s got a broken arm and a concussion! And it could’ve been much much worse. She could be a quadraplegic, or dead!’

‘But she isn’t, is she?’

‘You’re damn lucky she isn’t! Where are you calling from? The police station?’

‘No. They had to let me go. Couldn’t pin me. Mr Owens has mighty fine lawyers.’

Christine paused. She felt sick with anger. She whispered hoarsely, ‘Why did you do it?’

‘I’m not saying I did, but if I did, it would be to scare you into selling Dancer.’

‘You almost killed my daughter? To scare us into selling a … a horse? I can’t believe I’m hearing this!’ Mousie was standing beside Christine listening raptly to every word, her eyes wide with curiosity. Christine went on. ‘Then why did you steal him last night? If you thought you’d scared us into selling him?’

‘Insurance, Mrs James? To show you we’re serious? To be in a better bargaining position? Pick your reason and name a price. Mr Owens will pay just about anything at this point. Then you’ll have nothing to worry about, and I can get on with other things. Do us all a favour.’

‘We are not interested in selling Dancer. Mr Owens can have any other horse in the world. Tell him to speak to me directly instead of sending you to do his bidding. I’m warning you now that the police will not let you continue to persecute us. Stop this craziness now, before there’s a tragedy.’ She slammed the phone down into the receiver.

Christine had to sit down. Her face was white and tense, her hands were trembling.

'Mom, what's wrong? What did he say?' Mousie was alarmed.

'Mousie, think carefully. If we don't sell them Dancer, this ... this horror will continue. I want you to think it over and tell me what you want to do.'

'You're asking me if I'd sell Dancer to people who kidnap horses? I couldn't live with myself. No, Mom, I don't even have to think about it. He's not for sale.' Mousie was definite and firm. 'I always thought Mr Owens was strange, but now I wonder if he's actually insane.'

Christine took a long look at her child. Remarkable girl, she thought.

'Okay, Mousie. But it's not over. Mr Owens and Chad Smith will try something again, even after the police warning last night. They might be a bit more cautious, but this phone call proves they still want Dancer. Nevertheless, we'll have to get on with our lives. Business as usual. We'll have to be extra careful, but worrying won't solve anything.'

'Except cause warts.' Christine looked at her daughter, and slowly started to laugh. Mousie joined in and they gave each other a big hug. Whatever was to come, they would face it head-on, and together.

Sandy Casey drove his little red Sunbird convertible over to Hogscroft the next day. His parents had paid for half the car, and he had earned the remainder with various summer jobs. He was very proud of the second-hand car, and he'd chosen it with care. Before leaving his house, he'd shined it up and polished the wheels and vacuumed the interior. He even sprayed it with room freshener. It looked and smelled like new.

'Are you trying to impress someone?' his ten-year-old sister Rosalyn had teased. 'It still looks like an old clunker to me.'

'You'd really get to me if I cared what you think,' Sandy had replied in the offhand way of brothers.

Sandy had wondered if he should call Hilary first. He liked her, but couldn't decide if he should drop in or not. He was in a dilemma.

He sought out his father. He'd found him preparing the garden for winter in a pensive, distracted mood. Rory had listened, then told him 'nothing ventured, nothing gained'. That was enough encouragement for Sandy, and now he found himself behind the wheel of his pride and joy, turning into Hogscroft.

He stopped in front of the vine-covered stone house and took a deep breath. It had been far too cold to have the roof down and his ears were freezing, but the car looked better that way, he thought. He got out and walked up to the door and knocked. He looked at his watch. It was two o'clock, carefully chosen so that they'd be home from church if they went, and finished lunch, but lots of time before dinner. Pepper was barking inside the house. He knocked again. Their truck was outside so they must be home.

Mousie watched Sandy's car pull in from her upstairs window. She panicked, trying to think of some way to make herself look presentable. Her right arm was the arm she used to put on make-up. She felt frustrated and helpless.

'Mom! Help! Sandy's here and I look awful! Help me!'

Christine ran into her room, then stopped and said, 'Mousie, pull yourself together. I'm going to let the poor boy in and you're going to come down and greet him.'

'Why didn't he warn me? I look awful!'

'Don't be silly. You look fine.' Smiling to herself, Christine turned and left the room.

'Mom!'

Christine sighed and turned back, unable to leave her daughter in distress. Quickly she helped Mousie out of her old raggedy sweater, brushed her hair, and gave her a swift kiss on the top of her head. 'Now, you choose what you want to wear while I let him in. Call me if you need help. He's going to think no one's home!'

Sandy was thinking of leaving. Coming here was a mistake. Hilary probably was sleeping and recovering from her accident. And he'd promised Sara Preston he'd drop in that afternoon. He was turning to go just as Christine opened the door. His aftershave almost knocked her over.

'Why, Sandy. How nice to see you. Please come in.'

Sandy walked in and stood awkwardly in the hall.

'Have a chair, Sandy. I'll call Mousie. She'll be surprised to see you.'

Sandy sat. 'Thanks, Mrs James. I was driving around and found myself in the area, so I dropped in. I hope it's all right.'

'It's always nice to see you,' Christine said warmly. She meant it. He was a really nice boy. 'Mousie! You have company.'

Mousie appeared at the doorway. She'd managed to change into a deep red T-shirt and over it, her favourite dark green cable-knit v-neck sweater. Christine thought she looked tired but lovely, with or without the prominent snow-white sling.

'Hi, Sandy.'

He stood up. 'Do you want to go for a ride, Hilary? It's a little cold, but it's sunny, and I can put the heater on.'

'Okay. That'd be great. Okay, Mom?' Mousie seemed to be slightly flushed.

Christine smiled. 'Sure, that's fine. Now you two drive carefully. And wear your seatbelts!' She had a little lump in her throat as she watched them drive away. Her little baby was growing up.

She sighed as she went back to work on her bills and accounts. It didn't look very good for the roof. She'd get George to patch it again, and hope for the best. She'd have to extend her loan again, too. That didn't make her too happy. She prayed that the real estate market would pick up before she got seriously in debt. She pushed aside the recurring worry of how to pay for university for Mousie. That was coming soon enough.

Since Peter's death, Christine's mother had offered to help with expenses. Christine had stubbornly refused. She knew her mother didn't have a lot of money. Joy Featherstone would be delighted to help with her granddaughter's education, but Christine promised herself that it would only be a last resort. She focused her mind on her book-keeping.

There was a knock on the door. Christine hushed Pepper and went to see who was there. It was Rory. Wind-burned and handsome. She opened the door.

'Rory! Hi!' Christine was about to invite him in when he interrupted, strangely desperate.

'Christine, I know I shouldn't have come to you. But there's nowhere else I'd rather be.' Christine looked puzzled. 'I was outside working and I kept thinking about you. And me. I can't get you out of my mind. Can I come in?'

'I don't think so, Rory,' she said slowly. Christine could feel the tears rush to her eyes. She thought he was a friend, and that was safe. This wasn't.

'Christine, it's not what it seems, I really care about you. Can I please explain?'

'Rory, you're a married man. I can't hear this. It hurts me.'

'I mishandled things completely. Let me start again.'

'You are my friend, Rory. Please can we leave it like that?'

Rory started to speak, but realized that anything he said would sound contrived. He looked at Christine, principled and strong and good. She was so appealing to him. What could he say without appearing to be making excuses for being there? How could he have blundered so badly? Why had he been so sure she'd take him in her arms and comfort him? That was why he'd come, and he felt ashamed of himself.

He drew himself up. 'I'm sorry. I'll go now. I apologize for my impulsiveness.' Rory turned, went to his car, and without a backward glance, he disappeared.

Christine crumpled. She allowed herself to cry as she hadn't cried in years. She was disappointed and confused and totally crushed. What must he think of her? She felt that she'd lost a dear friend, and the loss was deep. At the same time, she knew that she would have loved to invite him in and take her chances. She wasn't proud of that. She went back to her bills, drained and unhappy, only to find that she couldn't quite face them.

Two hours later, Mousie flung open the door and bounded in.

'Mom! Mom! I can't believe it! I'm so happy! Sandy's going to pick me up every day and take me to school and drive me home. Oh, I think I'm going to die, and float around in heaven, I'm so happy!' With her one good arm, she swept her mother around the room and caught her up in her joy.

'Mousie, that's wonderful.'

'And Mom, I just know that he's going to ask me to the formal! He asked if I thought I'd go.'

'Really? And what did you say?'

'I said I hadn't given it much thought, and he said I should think about it!'

'Well then, when he asks you, we'll have to find a pattern and fabric and we'll make you the nicest dress at the dance.'

'Mom, I'll look around tomorrow and see what I want, then we'll work on a fabulous new me!'

'You're fabulous enough as you are. Now, before you get your coat off, let's go feed those neglected animals. Dancer needs extra love these days, while your arm heals. He's used to being ridden every day.'

Mousie excitedly waited for Sandy to pick her up for school the next morning. Her confidence was soaring, and she'd chosen her clothes carefully. She stood at the kitchen window, looking for him and thinking about how her whole status at school was about to change.

Wait till Sara and Carol-Ann see me with Sandy! They'll be totally green with envy! They'll have to treat me like a person now, instead of a piece of dirt. The Country Mouse, ha! And I'll be so sweet to them! They'll keep wondering when the axe will fall. Sandy's the most popular guy at school. And such a lot of fun. And so nice. And handsome. I can't believe he's going to ask me to the dance!

She could hardly contain herself when she saw the red glint of Sandy's car turn into the lane, with the roof up to keep out the cold winds.

'Bye, Mom! See you later!'

'Bye, Mousie. Have a good day!'

'A good day? This'll be the best day of my entire life!' she called as she threw on her coat and dashed out the door.

She stopped dead. There, in the passenger seat sat Sara Preston, her make-up perfect, long curly blond hair tousled, and a sneer on her face that would enrage a saint. She rolled down her window and said, 'You'll have to squeeze into the back, honey. And you can be the first to hear. Sandy and I are going to the formal together! Isn't that great?'

Mousie's legs turned to jelly and her stomach did a flip. She looked at Sandy. She could see from the expression on his face that she hadn't disguised her emotions one bit. He looked totally bewildered. She wanted to be swallowed up by the earth. And Sara looked for all the world like a giant cat with a bowl of warm cream.

'I don't think I need a ride today, but thanks for stopping,' she managed to say before running into the house.

'Whatever,' Sara snorted, as Sandy pulled out of the drive.

Later that morning Christine drove Mousie up to the front of the school. Mousie's tears had dried. Her face was less puffy, but there was no doubt in her mind that everyone at school would know she'd been crying.

'Mom, I've changed my mind. I can't go in there.'

'Take three deep breaths and plough in, honey. Sara wins if you don't show up. She'll be unbearable.'

'Right.' Mousie took her three deep breaths and without a backward glance, strode through the front doors.

'That's my girl,' Christine muttered through the lump in her throat. She suppressed the urge to protect her daughter from Sara and all other evil.

Mousie got her books from her locker, checked in with the office, and joined her class. The first person who caught her eye was Sandy. He smiled.

She looked down at her desk. Forget him, she told herself. There are lots of other fish in the sea. It's always darkest before the dawn. Who am I trying to fool, she thought. He's the greatest guy I know and I'd die to go out with him.

She deftly avoided him when the bell rang to change classes. Scuttling along head down, books clasped to her chest, she felt someone walking beside her. The person's shoes were shiny black patent leather, and clicked with every step. Mousie lifted her head and met the batting blue eyes of Sara Preston.

'I think I'll wear a low-cut dress, and I'd pictured floor-length with a slit all the way up one leg, but a mini would show off my legs better, so it's a really tough decision. What are you wearing, Mouse?'

'I'm not sure. Something that would complement my full-length black mink evening cape and diamond tiara.'

'OOh! So we do have nails! I suppose I wouldn't go if I were you, either, without a date. You'd just sit alone all night, nursing your broken arm.'

'Thanks, Sara. So nice chatting.'

'And I was so insensitive asking about a dress! I'm so sorry I asked.' With a sugar-coated smile, Sara disappeared down the hall.

Mousie leaned against the nearest locker and prayed for the strength to get through this horrible, embarrassing day.

Chapter 5

Samuel Owens

MONTHS WENT BY. It was early February and the snow was deep and sparkling white at Hogscroft. The sun was making an appearance and Dancer snorted and rolled in the snow. His coat had fully recovered its chestnut beauty. He was looking forward to Mousie riding him when she returned from school. Her arm had completely healed.

Sandy had phoned a couple of times after the formal fiasco, but Mousie had kept her distance, protecting her pride. Sandy's friendliness had fooled her once, and she didn't want that to happen again. Mousie had spent the night of the prom scrubbing tack and oiling leather. She'd shined up the entire barn and all the animals in it, in an effort to distract herself from thoughts of Sandy and Sara. The only outward signs of distress were the dust-caked tear marks on her face.

Mousie was now called Hilary by everyone but her mother. She was getting A's at school, was involved with the basketball team and the drama club, and had made a couple of friends who were strong enough to defy Sara Preston and Carol-Ann. Things were going well for her.

Christine had seen Rory only occasionally since the fall. The embarrassment between them was slowly disappearing, and a courteous friendship of sorts had re-emerged.

They'd never relaxed their vigil since the Queen's Exhibition. A spooky sense of being watched tarnished the atmosphere at Hogscroft, no matter how hard they tried to go on with their lives. The police were still putting together the case against Samuel Owens and Chad Smith, impeded at every turn by Sam's lawyers. It was difficult to prove that Dancer had been stolen from Hogscroft, since they'd denied knowledge of Dancer ever being at Owens stables, and all traces of the black dye had disappeared. Chad Smith vowed up and down that it was all a case of mistaken identity, and that he'd called the police on an honest mistake. And except for the word of the little boy Patrick Flanders, the police had trouble placing Chad Smith at the scene of the girth-snipping. Mack Jones was persisting however, and insisted that charges were pending, but progress was slow. Chad had been careful, nonetheless, to stay clear of Hogscroft.

Christine put down the phone. Another family looking for a country retreat. She looked at the winter wonderland out her window. Just yesterday there was mud and slush and grey skies. A good snowfall is a wonderful thing, she thought.

She pulled on her boots and her jacket and was about to leave to get the mail, when the phone rang. 'Probably work,' she mumbled, deliberating on whether or not to answer. She resigned herself to it and picked up the phone.

'Hello?'

'Christine James,' a woman's voice drawled.

'Speaking.'

'I'm a friend of Helena Casey's. Look, I'll make this short. She's been cheating on Rory for years. He won't look at me, Lord knows I've tried. He's always had a thing for you. That's why Helena won't give him a divorce. She's a dog in a manger. She hates you and considers you the competition. Thought you should know.' The woman laughed in a bored, unhappy way. 'Must run, but had to call. I feel much better now.'

Christine was reeling. Who was this woman? What was true, what was vicious slander? What could she do about it, anyway? Put it out of your mind, Christine, she chided herself. A glimmer of excitement flickered through her thoughts. Maybe? .... no. This woman is a shark, not to be listened to.

She calls herself a friend of Helena's! Helena sure doesn't need enemies.

Christine went to collect the mail, still whirling from the strange call, fighting with her emotions. Pepper bounced along in the snow beside her. The smell of earth was just under the surface, sending a message of hope for an early spring. Christine decided to have a walk to clear her head, and she strode off, Pepper delightedly jumping up and grabbing at her gloves.

Cheeks flushed and feeling better for the walk, Christine grabbed the mail on her way back, calling hello to her animals. As always, Charlie baa-ed his greeting and Dancer came over for a pat. 'Everybody tells me that you should be locked up. Good luck to me if I ever tried!' Dancer walked with her to the door, bowed, and ran off. He never ceased to amaze her.

She looked through the mail, sorting bills and junk mail. But what was this? Another letter with the royal seal! Mousie's going to be thrilled, Christine thought. How unexpected!

Mousie had barely stepped off the school bus when Christine opened the door and called, waving the letter, 'Mousie! Another royal letter!'

Mousie paused for a second, then raced into the house. She tore open the letter, not pausing even to say hello, and began to read aloud.

February 4th

Miss Hilary James,

The Queen has asked that I extend an invitation to Mrs Christine James, yourself, and Daring Dancer, to visit England in the second or third week of March. The Royal Family will be gathering at that time at Highgrove, the country home of Prince Charles.

Her Royal Majesty was so taken with you and your horse that she wishes to show you off to her family at a small, select horse show.

We will take the liberty of making all the arrangements. Please contact me at 789-5643 with your availability, and we will confirm a date.

Her Majesty is awaiting your reply.

Yours,
Andrew Chalmers, Brigadier

'This is too much! Holy!'

'Mousie, do you want to go?'

'Yes! Yes, I do! This is like a dream! She said in her get-well note that she might do this, but I never in a million years thought she meant it! England! Oh, this is great!' She danced around the room in glee, Christine laughing in pleasure. Mousie raced out the door to tell Dancer, calling back, 'Mom, nothing normal ever happens around here!'

February passed and the trip to England was now only a few weeks away. They still had some conditioning to do. Mousie's arm was perfect, but she still wasn't in the kind of shape she'd been in before her fall. Mousie was spending all her spare time working with Dancer.

She and Dancer had to walk down the road every day to use a neighbour's arena, because the footing wasn't good with the snow and ice in the outdoor ring.

One day, Sandy turned up at the arena. Mousie was completely taken by surprise. She smiled tensely at him and continued tightening the girth, promising herself that she'd keep her cool.

'Can I help with fallen bars and keep you company?' he asked.

'If you want.' Mousie got on Dancer's back from the mounting block.

'You don't mind if I'm here, do you?' Sandy wasn't sure how to make conversation with her.

'No, not at all.' She started her warm-up trots and canters and figure-eights. Soon, she forgot all about Sandy, and engrossed herself in the pleasure of riding this equine athlete.

They did a series of seven jumps at an average height of three feet, an easy task for Dancer.

Sandy raised the jumps to three-foot-six-inches on Mousie's instructions, and again to three-foot nine. Over the course they went again. Clean as a whistle.

When they were done, Sandy started to applaud. 'Bravo! Bravo!'

Mousie couldn't stay cool in the face of his appreciation. She smiled her infectious grin and nodded her thanks.

Not to be outdone, Dancer did his trademark bow. Sandy and Mousie laughed. 'Show-off!' said Mousie.

When the workout was finished and Mousie had cooled Dancer out and dismounted, Sandy asked, 'Can I walk you home?'

'That'd be nice. I mean if you have nothing to do.' She couldn't resist adding, 'And if Sara wouldn't mind.'

'What's that all about, Hilary? Sara and I aren't dating.'

'She seems to think so.'

'Well, I mean, we've gone out a few times, but it isn't serious.'

'Oh.'

'Hilary, you don't understand.'

'Understand what?'

'I don't know. You act so snotty to me. And I like you. But you confuse me. Do I bug you or something?'

'No!' Mousie gasped, then regained her composure. 'But I don't want to bug Sara, either. She's very possessive of you, and I don't want to, uh, I don't know, Sandy. You confuse me, too.'

'Come on, let's start home. It's getting dark. We can talk on the way.'

'But what about your car?'

'I'll just walk back and get it. No big deal.'

They started out for Hogscroft, and talked as they walked.

'Hilary, when are you leaving for England?'

'How did you know I was going to England?'

Sandy smiled. 'I listen with interest when the gossip is about you. I heard it at school. So, when do you go?'

'We're taking off on the twelfth of March.'

'That'll be fun. Good luck, right-ho and all that.'

Mousie snorted at his fake English accent. 'Thanks.'

'Did you know my dad has a thing for your mother?'

'Huh? What do you mean, Sandy? What about your mom?'

Shaking his head, he answered, 'They should've had a divorce years ago. They've only stayed together for Ros and me, though I don't know why. But my mom really doesn't like being around him, and you can imagine how awful it is. My dad always tries to make things work, but there's nothing there.'

'I'm sorry, Sandy. I had no idea.'

'Most people don't. I just thought you and I should be friends. I mean, in case your mom and my dad get married or something.'

'Get married? What are you talking about?'

'My dad'd marry her in a second. I think he's always carried a torch for her, as they used to say.'

'This is a shock. I don't know what to say.'

'Nothing new there. You don't normally talk to me at all.'

'What? I don't mean not to, I mean, I want to talk to you, but …'

'Hey, don't worry about it, I was kidding.'

'I don't know when you're kidding and when you're not.'

'I guess I'm sort of serious. You ignore me at school. I thought we were friends after the whole Queen's Exhibition thing. Then suddenly, you act like we're strangers.'

'I thought we were friends, too. But when you showed up

in your car with Sara after asking me if I … well, anyway, she's not exactly my greatest fan.'

'What's with that, anyway? She always acts like she's mad at you or something.'

'I wish I knew.'

'She's nice to me, that's all I know, and she's real pretty. She asks me out, and I go when I've got nothing else to do. It's as simple as that. And there's nothing between us.' Sandy looked at Mousie and shrugged. His smile disarmed her.

Mousie wasn't sure why Sandy was telling her this, and she struggled against admitting that she was pleased.

When Mousie didn't respond, Sandy said, 'I'll miss you while you're gone.'

'I'll bet,' answered Mousie crisply, imagining him rushing over to Sara's house the minute he left. She remembered all too well how she'd been humiliated before.

Hearing her cool response, Sandy felt so stupid he blushed. He was glad that the dusk masked his fiery complexion. 'Well, here's your lane. I'll go back and get my car. Oh. Good luck in England. You'll be great.' And he was off like a rabbit.

'Sandy!' Mousie called out.

Sandy spun around. 'Yes?'

'Thanks.' Then she whispered, unheard, 'And I'll miss you, too.' An unbidden tear slipped down her cheek. What was wrong with her? Why couldn't she have a decent conversation with Sandy? Dancer nickered and nudged her, trying to cheer her up. When that didn't work, he knelt down and pushed her with his nose until she got on his back. A sad girl and a sympathetic horse walked together down the country road toward home.

Christine had been on the phone all that day. Roof repairs, travel arrangements, her mother to look after Hogscroft while they'd be gone, real estate dealings, a load of boring but essential details. She had to get out of the house.

Throwing on her coat and boots, she put the answering machine on, and left. She walked past the barn, calling to Mousie and Dancer, who'd just returned, 'I'm going for a walk. A long walk! See ya!'

She strode along at a good clip. Pepper raced to catch up when she noticed that Christine had gone without her. She should've worn a hat. It was getting cold. And gloves. Her mind started to open in the outside air. Her heart lifted to the setting sun, the purply dimming skies, the freshness. It felt good to be outside after her day on the end of the telephone wires.

She was just thinking of turning back with her head bent down to ward off the north wind. She almost walked right into the bulky form of Samuel Owens. He'd stopped his car when he spotted her and was deliberately standing in her way. Pepper warned Christine of his presence one step before collision.

'Mrs James.' He spoke in a jovial, deep voice.

'Mr Owens!'

'How lovely to bump into you like this. You're looking well.'

'Thank you.' Christine stared, on guard.

'How have you been?'

'Fine, thank you.' She didn't quite know how to take this. He seemed different than she'd expected. More friendly.

'Mrs James ... may I call you Christine?'

'Of course.'

'And please call me Sam. I grew up with your mother, you know. We went through school together.'

'I know. She told me.'

'Christine, I want to apologize to you for the actions of an employee of mine, Chad Smith.'

'What do you mean?' Christine eyed him suspiciously.

'The police filled me in on everything that's gone on, and

I'm aghast. I should've spoken to you sooner, but until recently, I had no real idea what he was up to.'

'Just a minute, here. You didn't instruct him to do what he did?'

Owens laughed sadly. 'Of course not! Sure, I wanted to buy your lovely animal, but I'd never authorize anything like stealing, or cutting a girth! Surely you never believed that I ...' He sounded amazed that Christine could have such a thought. 'But you did think that, didn't you? That's what I was worried about.'

'Well, I have to admit, Mr Owens ...'

'Please. Call me Sam.'

'Okay, Sam. Yes, I assumed that you were behind the things that Chad did. He works for you. It seems logical that you ...'

Owens looked very sad. He looked straight into her eyes and interrupted, 'Christine, I hope you'll believe me when I tell you this. I wanted Dancer, yes. In fact, I wanted to take him all the way to the Olympics, something that you unfortunately wouldn't be able to afford. I asked Chad to approach you, yes. But the rest; the girth, the threats, the stealing; he did himself. He probably thought I would be pleased with him if he obtained Dancer for me. The methods were his own invention. It sickens me to think about it. I had no idea how crazy he'd become. I fired him, of course, when I found out. I truly hope that now you'll understand.'

'You fired him? Well, I'm glad you spoke to me about this, Sam. I really feel a lot better knowing it's only Chad we have to worry about, and now that he's fired, he won't have any reason to want Dancer. I guess there's nothing to worry about at all.' She smiled.

'I should have contacted you sooner. So sorry. Of course you know that my offer to purchase still stands. Any time. For any price.'

'We'll never sell Dancer, Sam. He means too much to my daughter. I hope you understand.'

'Of course. No means no.' He smiled at his little joke.

Pepper had been growling, and now, unable to restrain herself any longer, she jumped at Owens' coat and hung on.

'Pepper, down! What's got into you? Down! Oh, Sam, I'm so sorry!'

Rory Casey was driving home in the dusk, when he saw a man talking to a woman beside a car on the road. He was almost past when he noticed the small dog attached to the man's sleeve, and the woman trying to pry it off. Then he twigged who they were. He stopped his car and came up beside Christine.

'Samuel Owens,' he said. 'Nice night for a walk.'

'Rory Casey. Good to see you, neighbour. Well, I must be off. Nice talking with you, Christine.'

'Pepper, down!' Reluctantly, the little Jack Russell dropped to the ground, but growled until Samuel Owens had gotten into his car. Christine waved goodbye, her mind full of new thoughts. Rory shook his head.

'What was that all about?'

'It seems I may have been wrong about Mr Owens. He apologized to me for what Chad did. He says he didn't know what Chad was up to, and when he found out, he fired him. In fact, he seems like a very nice man.'

'Pepper isn't fooled.'

'Is it possible that you've been unjustly hard on him, too?'

'Let me put it this way. When I saw you here with Owens, I stopped to rescue a damsel in distress.'

'Why, thank you, Sir Galahad.'

'My pleasure. Like a lift back?'

'That'd be great. It sure got dark fast.'

Pepper jumped in first and sat on the front seat between them.

There was an awkward silence for a minute, then they both spoke at once.

'I hear that you're …'

'I had an odd phone …'

They both laughed, and Rory said, 'Okay, you go first.'

'Actually, I'd rather you did. I've rethought saying what I was going to say.'

'Well, that does it. I was about to say that Sandy told me you and Hilary are off to England to perform for the royal family. Congratulations, but however great that is, anything that you decide not to say must be far more intriguing.' Rory was teasing, enjoying himself.

'Yes, we're going to England on the March break. Mousie's absolutely thrilled, and so am I.'

'Now, what was it that you weren't going to say? Tell me.'

Christine didn't quite know how to answer. She didn't want the mood to change to serious, but she couldn't think up anything else. 'I had an odd phone call last week. That's what I was about to say.'

'Oh, from whom?'

'Ah. She wouldn't say. A friend of Helena's.'

'A friend?' Rory frowned.

'Well, that's debatable. She wasn't very friendly, that's for sure.'

'Did she say anything … upsetting?' Rory was concerned.

'No! Don't worry,' Christine tried to sound light. 'She was just a gossip.'

Rory took a deep breath. 'It was about my marriage, wasn't it?'

'I don't believe everything I hear, Rory.'

'This time it's true.' He turned up Hogscroft's lane. 'Helena and I have been living together only for the sake of our children. It never was a fairy-tale marriage.'

'Rory, I'm sorry. I shouldn't have brought it up.'

'I'm glad you did. It helps explain my behaviour last fall. I hope you'll forgive me for blurting out my feelings that way.' He searched her face for encouragement. 'I've never forgotten what a good thing we had, those many years ago, before marriages and children. You've always remained in my heart. And then being around you for that short time over Mousie's accident, it came home to me how much I want you in my life again. And I want to be in your life.'

Christine had sat motionless. She was filled with emotion. 'Rory, I didn't know. I thought you and Helena were the perfect couple. I'm sorry about how it must've been for you. When you came to my door last fall, I only knew that I couldn't get involved with a married man. Any married man, even you.'

'I know that. And I didn't mean to put you in that position. I wasn't thinking straight. I've regretted it ever since.' He cleared his throat. This was difficult. 'I've been trying for some time now to get a divorce. The kids are suffering and it's no good. My lawyer is having some trouble with her, but it should be resolved soon.'

'I wish you luck with it, Rory. This can't be easy.'

'Christine, when it's all settled, can I call you?'

Her heart lurched. 'Yes, Rory. I'd like that.' Christine reached over and squeezed his hand. Rory wanted so much to kiss her. Christine could sense it.

'I'm going now. If I stay, there's no telling what might happen.' She kissed him quickly on the cheek, smiled warmly, and hopped out.

As Rory watched her racing up to the door followed by the bouncing Pepper, his whole body filled with happiness. He let out a little whoop of joy. Life looked a whole lot better.

Mousie was dreaming. Rain pelted down on a barren landscape, wind howling wildly. Lightning crashed, illuminating a beautiful woman with a blond chignon under a soaked riding hat with a torn veil. The woman was wearing a battered sidesaddle fox-hunting costume, the long black skirts covered in mud. A tattered white frill showed at the velvet collar of her black jacket, and her face was badly scratched and bleeding. Blood dripped onto the blouse and blurred into pink with the rain. Her beseeching eyes seemed to be trying to communicate something important, and her lips moved, forming words. She was speaking urgently, but to no avail. Mousie tried as hard as she could, but couldn't hear. The wind continued, ever louder, screaming and wailing, obscuring the words.

Mousie awoke, her heart pounding, to the sound of Pepper whining. That's what made the wind howl in my dream, she thought. It was pitch black. She pulled the pillow over her ears, trying to get back to sleep. The little dog whined again, and jumped onto Mousie's bed, licking her face. Mousie lifted her covers and said, 'Get back in here, Pepper, it's cold without you. And it's too early to get up.' She peeked at the glowing numbers on her clock. Four in the morning. Pepper increased her urgency and pulled on the blankets with her teeth.

'All right! Didn't you pee before you went to bed?' Mousie grumbled as she put on her slippers and fleecy yellow housecoat and started down the stairs. Pepper ran to the door and barked. 'Pepper! Shh! You'll wake Mom.'

Mousie opened the door. Pepper raced out toward the barn, barking at the top of her voice. A dim light illuminated the barn windows. Alarmed, Mousie grabbed her coat and followed. Pepper continued to bark, and Mousie could hear a symphony of sounds. Charlie baa-ing, geese hissing, Pepper yelping, and Dancer's hooves crashing on wood. He was thrashing hard.

She slowed as she neared the barn door. What am I doing? I could get myself killed! Suddenly, the barking stopped. Mousie froze. What happened to my dog? she thought. She stepped onto the mounting block under a window, and looked in. Chad Smith. Syringe in hand. Pepper snarling, with her jaws clenched on his leg. Dancer agitated, tied up with a twitch on his nose and a cloth tied over his eyes.

She couldn't just stand by. She had to do something. She picked up the shovel that was propped up against the wall and charged into the barn, caution thrown to the wind, and loudly commanded, 'You put that thing down!'

Chad started. Composing himself, he turned to her and smiled, 'What do you think is in this syringe? Any guesses? Orange juice?'

'Put it down! Don't you dare touch that horse!'

'Pure death, that's what's in here. Death for all animals, big and small.' He looked down at the dog clinging onto him with every fibre in her body, and brought the syringe to her neck.

'No!' Mousie swung the shovel and knocked the syringe out of his hand. 'Down, Pepper! Get Mom!' The Jack Russell dropped, and stared at Mousie, not understanding. 'Get Mom! Go home!' Hearing the word 'home', Pepper bounced out the door and was gone.

The syringe lay on the floor directly behind Dancer. Mousie held the shovel up, braced to hit Chad if he moved.

'So now what? You saved your dog, but now it's just you and me. You really shouldn't have come here.' He stepped closer to Mousie. She noticed that the geese and Charlie were locked in a stall.

'Are you crazy? Why are you doing this?'

'Actually, this is a mercy killing. He's a dangerous horse. He tried to kill me.' He looked very nervous. He repeatedly licked his lips.

Mousie was scared. Was he on drugs? She tried to reason with him.

'But I thought you liked Dancer. You wanted to buy him.'

'My boss wanted to buy him. And you wouldn't sell him. It's made my life very, very difficult. You deprived Mr Owens of his dream, and he's not too happy about that. He wanted Sara to win Olympic gold for him on this horse, but you wouldn't sell. And if he can't have this horse, nobody should. That's why he wants him dead. And that's what I'm here to do.'

He made a sudden dash for the syringe, diving clumsily to the floor and grabbing it. Mousie, in an effort to make him drop it, hit blindly at him with all her strength, smashing into his thighs with the shovel.

At the same time Dancer, still blindfolded, lashed out with both rear legs. His back right knocked Chad on the shoulder, and with a terrified scream the man fell onto the syringe. It pierced the skin of his chest, sending the deadly serum straight into his bloodstream.

Chad Smith's eyes bugged in amazement. His jaw jutted out, and his mouth widened into a grimace. He grunted. He gasped horribly, his body going rigid, then wheezed loudly as he tried to inhale. The whine of the wheeze lost volume, then stopped altogether. He went limp, then thumped down, face first. A couple of seconds passed. His body shuddered spastically, then it was still. He was dead.

Mousie stared. She could hardly breathe. Her legs were threatening to collapse. Her head was spinning. Her stomach lurched. She couldn't move.

Dancer nickered, releasing her from the spell. She staggered into the closest stall and vomited. He nickered again, more impatiently. She struggled to her feet, and rinsed herself with water from the tap outside the stall.

She then quickly attended to Dancer. She removed his blindfold, unwound the nose-twitch and untied him. She wrapped her arms around his neck and held him. All her limbs were shaking. Mousie thought with a great pang of her father. How she wished he were there. Yet, somehow she thought maybe he was.

Dancer pushed himself from her arms, turned around and sniffed at the body. He shook his head and snorted.

The door swung open and Pepper dashed in and slid to a stop. Christine came running at full tilt with Peter's old hunting rifle ready to shoot.

'Mousie!' she cried. She stopped. She slowly took in the scene. It was horrible. 'Honey, are you all right?'

She put down the rifle, ran to Mousie, and hugged her daughter fiercely, her eyes glistening with emotion. 'You can tell me what happened later. Right now, we must go to the house. I have to call an ambulance. Immediately. And the police.' They quickly moved toward the house, Christine supporting her shocked daughter, Dancer and Pepper following.

The ambulance arrived within minutes. Mousie and Christine watched from the house while the crew attended to their business. Mack Jones was on his way. Pepper was crunching on dog food, proud of the role she'd played. Dancer stayed close to the house, munching the hay that Christine had put out for him, and keeping a wary eye on the barn.

Christine waited for the sobs and shakes to subside, and listened in horror to the story as Mousie sipped at her hot chocolate in between broken sentences. This is incomprehensible, Christine thought. Greed makes such monsters of us. Was Owens sick, as Chad had told Mousie? Or, if what Owens had told her on the road was true, Chad Smith had been the sick one. Christine shuddered. She was very confused. It was difficult to fathom the enormity of what had just occurred.

As they stood at the window, arms linked, headlights appeared up the lane.

'That's Mack. Mousie, why don't you stay here where it's warm, and I'll go talk to him.'

As Christine was bundling up, another set of headlights followed the first.

'Mom! That's Sandy's car! And his Dad's here, too.'

As the Caseys got out of their car, Rory gave his son instructions.

'Go in the house, Sandy. Make Mousie some tea, and try to

take her mind off all this.' Rory walked to meet Christine, who was striding out toward him.

'It seems I'm nothing but trouble for you, Rory. You're thoughtful to come, but honestly, things are under control.'

'I know they are, Christine, but Mack called and I wanted to make sure you and Mousie were all right. After all, I am involved. Surely you haven't forgotten the black horse, "Spirit"!' Christine smiled at the reference, and Rory was pleased. He took her by the arm and they walked to the barn, where Mack was conferring with the paramedics.

'There was more than enough in that syringe to kill twenty horses,' the man was saying. 'He didn't have a chance. He died instantly.'

'So . . . final,' Christine whispered.

'Oh, yes. No question about that,' Mack answered. 'I suspect it was an overdose of barbiturate in the syringe. Probably Euthanyl or T 61. He wouldn't have felt any pain. Either one will kill a horse within ten seconds. The lab will determine formally at the autopsy.'

However much trouble Chad had made for them, and however much danger he'd put Mousie in, the finality of death awed Christine completely.

'I'm very sorry,' she said.

They watched as the body was removed. The paramedics completed their duties, and the ambulance drove off.

'Mack, will there be an investigation?' Rory was concerned.

'Well, it was an accident, pure and simple. But we'll have to get to the truth about why Smith was even here in the first place. And that means talking to Sam Owens first thing in the morning.' He smiled weakly. 'Which is in a couple of hours.'

'Right. You can probably expect some fancy dancing there.' Rory sounded sceptical.

Christine spoke up. 'He's innocent until proven guilty,

Rory. He told me that he fired Chad because he was doing these things, that Chad was crazy.'

'Leave it to me.' Mack gave Rory a quick glance, and put his pad and pencil into his coat pocket. 'Just consider yourself lucky that Mousie wasn't killed. She was in grave danger.'

Christine shivered. 'You're right. Thank you, Mack. You've been great.' She turned away, then realized she didn't want them to leave. She asked, 'Why don't we all go into the house? I'll make some fresh coffee.'

Rory checked his watch. 'I'm on. It's too late to go back to bed.'

'Super. That's just what I need. A good cup of coffee,' nodded Mack.

Around the cosy kitchen table, made cosier by the number of people, they ate bagels and cream cheese and jam and drank coffee, cocoa, and fresh orange juice. Everyone tried to keep the mood light, but the horrible events of the night were impossible to ignore. They took comfort in being together, after sharing the ordeal.

Mousie had told Sandy the whole story and felt somewhat better, but the image of Chad Smith on the barn floor was never far from her mind. Pepper had cuddled onto Mousie's lap and was sleeping contentedly, her job done. Christine poured another cup for those who wished it, and tears came to her eyes.

'Mom, what's wrong?' Mousie asked.

'I'm so grateful that you're alive, Mousie.' She held her daughter tightly to her bosom as finally the tears fell.

Ten o'clock that same morning, a long, shiny black limousine pulled up to the front of Hogscroft. Mousie saw it first, from her bedroom window, and called down to her mother.

'Mom! Someone's here! He's getting out of his car. It's Mr Owens! He's carrying something ... lots of things!'

'Don't stand there yelling! Come down and answer the

door, and tell him I'll be right there. I'm up to my elbows in suds.' She was giving Pepper a much-needed bath. She'd been rolling in horse manure.

Mousie rushed to the door, and opened it. Samuel Owens stood there, arms full of gifts.

'Hello, child, you must be the talented Hilary I've heard so much about. I'm Samuel Owens, a friend of your mother.'

'Pleased to meet you. Actually, I met you once with your niece, Sara, at a horse show. My mother will be here in a ...'

Before she could finish her sentence, a soapy Pepper bounded into the room, locking her teeth onto Owens' coat and dripping all over him.

'Pepper!' screamed Mousie. 'Get down!'

'Down, Pepper! Bad dog!' Christine appeared at the doorway, splattered in soap and water. She dove for Pepper, grabbed her, and took her to the basement.

'Mr Owens, are you all right?' asked Mousie.

'Yes, yes, don't worry. Your little dog and I don't get along, that's all. It's nothing.' He smiled reassuringly.

'Pepper's not usually like this.' Christine re-entered, wiping her hands on a towel. She passed another to Owens to brush off his coat.

'No apologies necessary. In fact, I'm here to apologize to you. Mack Jones called on me this morning with the tragic news about Chad Smith. I know I should've had the man put away, but he'd been a trusted employee for many years. I kept hoping he'd get better. I'm far too sentimental for my own good. And now, I feel totally responsible. When I fired him, he must have gone off the deep end. It could've been far, far worse, and it would've ultimately been my fault.'

Mousie and Christine just stared and listened. The man seemed so genuine, so kind. He couldn't have been behind the dreadful events of last night.

'Christine, Hilary, I feel terrible about this. You must've gone through hell because of Chad Smith. But please don't remember him too harshly. He was a very disturbed man.'

He indicated the table where he'd piled his bundles.

'I know nothing can possibly make up for what happened last night, but it would make me feel better if you'd accept these gifts in the spirit of forgiveness.'

Sam pulled the biggest bundle open to reveal great bunches of bright yellow spring daffodils. Christine smiled.

'Thank you, Sam, they're beautiful.'

He handed Mousie a large package, and Christine a smaller one. They opened them.

'Swiss chocolates!' squealed Mousie.

'Oh, Sam, this is too kind.' Christine held a jar of the finest Russian caviar.

'I'm glad you're pleased. Thank you for your understanding. I must be off now to console Chad's widow. But don't hesitate to call me if there's anything I can ever do for you. And I mean that sincerely.'

Samuel Owens left. Mousie and Christine were confused by the difference between the Sam Owens they feared and the Sam Owens that had just visited.

The indignant howling from the basement snapped them back into reality, and Mousie went to release Pepper from her prison.

Chapter 6

England

FEBRUARY GAVE WAY to March, and time was flying towards the date of their departure. Hogscroft was buzzing with preparations. Christine was frantic about what clothes to pack, what to patch up, what to sew. No money to buy new anything. What they had would have to do.

Mousie polished tack in the barn, repairing loose buckles, stitching broken leather. Dancer was exercised daily, and was fit as a fiddle.

Passports were in order, papers prepared for Dancer. Vaccinations, veterinary visits, all was done. March the twelfth, the date of departure, was the next day.

Christine was upstairs cramming her tired old clothes into a suitcase. Pepper started barking. The doorbell rang. She ran her fingers through her hair, descended the stairs and opened the door.

An attractive, chic young woman smiled brightly and said, 'Mrs James, my name is Amanda Silver. I'm a personal wardrobe consultant and I have something for you.' She turned and motioned to a man in a van, parked outside.

As the man came through the door, arms laden with bags, she said, 'These are gifts for you and your daughter, from an anonymous friend. Everything that suits is yours. Whatever you can't use, we'll return.'

By the man's second over-burdened trip, Christine had found her voice. She stammered, 'Oh, but I couldn't. This is too much. I shouldn't. Who sent these clothes?'

'Ah, that's a secret.' The woman shook her finger at

Christine. 'Now, try on all the clothes, shoes and accessories that appeal to you. Choose what you wish, and then give me a call. Here is my card. When you call, I'll send Herb back to retrieve what you're not keeping. Do you think you could decide by five o'clock this afternoon?'

'Yes. Certainly. Thank you, er, Amanda.' Christine's eyes were as wide as saucers as she stood in a stupor, watching the van disappear down the drive.

She sprang to life. 'Mousie! Get in here!'

'Mom, what did I do?' Mousie came in panting.

'Nothing! Look at all this. Start trying on clothes!'

Mousie was radiantly happy. Gorgeous new clothes. Beautiful new shoes. Everything from the best shops. This was incredible! She tried on pants, sweaters, skirts, shoes, jackets, all perfect for their trip. There was even an assortment of coats and gloves.

'These cost a fortune. Put the things you can't live without on that chair,' said Christine, 'We can't keep everything.'

'But it's all so beautiful!' Mousie cried.

'But it's all so expensive. We'll keep only a few things, because I'm going to insist on paying for them. Somehow. Eventually. My guess is that this is your grandmother's idea. Everything fits perfectly, even the shoes. Who else would have known our shoe sizes? She must have hired Amanda to select an assortment of appropriate clothes for our trip. This is just the sort of thing she'd do.' She had a thought. 'Have you spoken to her recently?'

'Don't blame me! I didn't tell her we needed new clothes!'

'I'm not suggesting that you did. I'm just trying to figure it out.'

In the end, after sorting and making difficult decisions, the two women each had a co-ordinated mix-and-match ensemble that would take them anywhere. Christine's were in golds and greens and tweeds with creamy blouses. Mousie's were more dramatic with black and reds and purples with crisp white blouses. Each had a jacket with corresponding pants and two skirts, one long to be worn with boots, one short to go with shoes. Two blouses; one dressy, one plain. Two sweaters, to alter the moods of the ensembles. Silk scarf, wool scarf, gloves, tams. Dress shoes, walking shoes, boots. And all topped by a good wool coat; dark green tweed with a brown suede collar for Christine, belted black-and-white houndstooth for Mousie.

They were delirious. 'What about all the other stuff, Mom? Shouldn't we reconsider? We don't want to insult Gran by rejecting her gifts!'

'Good try, honey. I'm calling Amanda before you go crazy with greed.' She picked up the business card that the woman had given her.

'But it's not nearly five o'clock!'

Christine smiled. 'The sooner they're gone, the less the temptation.'

'Mom, you're no fun at all.' Mousie chortled with glee as she swept her new clothes up in her arms and spun around.

Herb arrived with the van just as they'd finished repackaging the things they were returning. He produced brand new luggage with a flourish as he walked in the door. Big suitcases with matching carry-ons. Mousie chose the black and Christine chose the tan. It felt like the very best Christmas in the world.

'Packing is going to be fun,' Mousie sighed, 'for the first time in my life!'

Christine sent Mousie upstairs to repack, and picked up the phone. She dialled her mother, Joy Featherstone.

'Hello?'

'Mom, you shouldn't have!'

'Christine. Whatever are you talking about?'

'You know perfectly well. They're beautiful, Mom, but I

know how much everything cost and I know you can't afford it. I'm going to pay you back.'

'You most certainly will not. I can spend my money any way I choose.'

'You're very thoughtful and generous, and we both look like millionaires. But I can't let you pay, it's far too much.'

'Enough, Christine! It'd make me very happy if you'd enjoy them.'

'Thank you, Mom. I mean it.'

'It's my pleasure, dear. It truly is. Let me do this for you and my dear Mousie.'

'Mom, you're great.'

'That's what mothers are for.'

'You're not an ordinary mother, and you know it. Thanks.'

'Stop thanking me! I'll see you tomorrow. Bye!'

The second they hung up, the phone rang. Christine picked it up.

'Hello?'

'Christine, it's Rory.'

'Hi, Rory!'

'Are you all packed and ready to go?'

'Actually, I'm just starting. My amazing mother sent over a whole new wardrobe! I can't believe it.'

'Aren't you lucky! Joy's terrific. I always got along with her. I was just calling to say goodbye and that I'll be thinking about you. The whole time you're gone. I hope you have a really good time.'

'Thanks, Rory. We will.'

'I'll miss you.'

'I'll miss you, too.'

Christine hung up the phone smiling broadly, and went upstairs to put her beautiful new wardrobe into her handsome new luggage. The Queen herself had never felt more royal.

The next afternoon, Christine's mother arrived. Joy Featherstone was a strong and cheerful person who had a positive attitude about things, and never passed an opportunity without seizing it. She was looking forward to spending some time in the country with her fluffy little sheepdog, Diva. Diva and Pepper always had mischievous fun together. Joy was good company, and Christine and Mousie loved her visits.

'Mom! It's so good to see you,' Christine called when she saw her mother and her dog get out of the ancient silver Lancia. 'Mousie, Gran is here!'

Mousie ran out to carry in her bags, and Joy gave her a big hug. Diva jumped up on Mousie to say hello then ran off in search of Pepper. Joy and Mousie were very fond of each other. Joy had always been important to her granddaughter, and even more so after the death of her father. 'You look beautiful, Mousie!'

'So do you, Gran! And thanks so, so, so much for those gorgeous clothes! They're absolutely perfect!' She looked her grandmother over. 'Did you get that coat and hat in Paris?'

'Actually, I bought them in Milan. But don't tell your mother, she thinks I waste my money on superficial things like clothes and travel. Which I do, but you only live once! You have an eye for quality, Mousie. You take after your old gran.' They had broad smiles on their faces as they walked into the house.

Christine and her mother embraced. 'Mom, you look wonderful as always. It's been too long since you came to visit.'

'You're busy people. And I've been travelling. But you're right dear, far too long.'

'Mousie, please take Gran's things to her room.'

'Thanks, Mousie,' called Joy as Mousie carried the suitcases up the stairs.

'Christine, how are you? Are things going better for Mousie at school, now? Tell me everything.'

'I'm fine, and Mousie's great. She's got a couple of good friends, and the other girls aren't bothering her so much. We're managing nicely, Mom. I can't tell you how much better life has been lately.'

'I'm so glad about Mousie. Girls can be such devils to each other. It's jealousy, you know. The blessing is that she'll be stronger for it. And she's a survivor, Christine, like you and me. The women in this family are made of good stuff.'

Joy sat down at the kitchen table and paused. She looked directly at her daughter, and said, 'Christine, I've been worried about all the trouble you've had with Sam Owens. I knew Sam in school, you know. He was always extremely strange.' Joy shuddered. 'The stories I could tell you ...'

'Don't be so quick to blame Sam Owens, Mom. He told me his man, Chad Smith, was crazy, and that he was acting on his own.' Christine was trying to keep things light. 'Anyway, it's all over now. Sam came here with flowers and gifts to apologize for Chad's actions, and he was very nice.'

'Nice is one thing Sam Owens most definitely is not. And don't assume it's over.' Joy was very earnest. 'Don't let his act fool you, Christine. In grade nine, he had two boys hold Joe Coldwater while he stripped the clothes off him with a filleting knife, and carved "RAT" into his chest. His father paid off the family and sent Sam off to boarding school to avoid the consequences.'

'That's horrible. But that happened a long time ago, Mom. He was a kid. People change.'

'He did it because Joe told the principal that it was Sam who'd beat the Clarence girl within an inch of her life and left her out in the schoolyard after dark. If the janitor hadn't taken the garbage out that night, she would've died of exposure.'

'Mom, I'm trying to put this behind me. Don't you see? I don't want to even think about Sam Owens.' Christine twisted her fingers together anxiously. 'I believe what you're telling me, and I think it's despicable. But you always said that people deserve a future no matter what their past.'

'Christine, listen to me. He's a dangerous man. He could never control his temper, and he always got what he wanted, however he had to do it. The Clarence girl had refused to date him. That was her sin. So he made sure she didn't date anyone else. And there are plenty more stories I could tell you. Don't underestimate him.'

'How can I, when people like you and Rory keep telling me?' Christine took a deep breath, and forced a lighter tone. She was very confused, and really didn't want a fight. 'Anyway, we'll be far away in England for the next week. Far from Samuel Owens, if it makes you feel better. Now, please, let's change the subject. I really don't feel like talking about him. I've had to deal with enough of this.' She looked beseechingly at her mother.

Joy wanted to make a comment, but she bit her tongue. She shrugged in defeat, and Christine sighed with relief.

Christine had put on the kettle and had been preparing tea and biscuits while they talked. 'It's good to have you here, Mom. I'm glad you can stay while we're gone.' She'd deliberately changed the subject.

'Christine, I'm delighted. It'll give me a welcome change of pace from the city.' Joy wasn't sure she'd made her point about Owens, but she knew better than to press. She'd try again later.

'Can you stay for a while when we get back?'

'A short visit, but I'd love to.'

'Wonderful. Now before I forget, here's the list of chores. Charlie, Pepper, the geese, odds and ends. Phone numbers in case of emergency. Neighbours, fire, police, all that stuff.' Joy looked over the list.

'Is Rory Casey the Rory you just mentioned? Is he still living around here?' Joy had spotted his name among the neighbours.

'You don't miss a thing, do you, Mom?'

'I like that boy. Always did. And darling, it's been almost three years now since our dear Peter died. Perhaps you should start thinking about your future. Christine, are you blushing?'

'I could never hide anything from you. Yes, I'm blushing. But Rory and I are just friends. He's married.'

'But you have some emotion for him?'

'Yes, but nothing's happening.'

'Best to keep it that way if he's married. Such a shame though. He's a dear boy.'

Mousie breezed in. 'Sandy told me that his dad's madly in love with Mom.' She'd heard the last part of the conversation from the hall, and couldn't resist. 'His parents are getting a divorce, and Sandy hopes that my mom and his dad'll get married.'

'Mousie!' cried Christine, truly amazed.

Joy laughed out loud. 'Well, well! I must remember to ask Mousie next time I want the whole story!'

Four o'clock that afternoon, Mousie and Christine gave their goodbyes to Pepper in the kitchen. 'We'll be back before you know it,' said Mousie. 'And Gran and Diva are here to keep you company.'

Christine cuddled the little dog, and gave her a kiss. 'You be good.'

Mousie laughed, 'Fat chance!'

Little Pepper knew they were leaving, and she put her head on her paws, looking up at them with very sad eyes.

Joy entered the room with Diva at her heels. Diva nudged Pepper with her nose and the two of them shot off around the house.

'Pepper'll be just fine,' Joy chuckled. 'She likes to milk the situation a bit, but I'm sure she'll survive.'

'Bye, Gran! See you next week.' Mousie and Joy hugged goodbye.

'You have fun, now. And show off that beautiful horse.'

'Thanks for looking after things, Mom,' said Christine, 'Have a good time.'

'I'll be cheering for you, dear,' Joy said to Mousie. 'Be careful, and have fun.' She waved goodbye as Mousie and Christine headed for the barn to get Dancer.

They opened the door to the barn, and Dancer nickered to them. He'd had a good feed, and was blanketed and booted. They led him outside and he quietly walked onto the old horse-trailer. 'A lesser horse would refuse to get on this thing,' said Mousie.

They carefully checked over everything, making sure they were totally prepared. Mousie's tack box and their new luggage were stowed in the back of the truck. They were ready to go.

The drive to the airport took less time than usual. Traffic was moving well.

Mousie talked non-stop. 'Mom, this is so exciting. Dancer seems to know that we're going somewhere special. I'm so happy I've got these new clothes. I look so much more sophisticated, don't you think? You look good, too, Mom. Isn't Gran great? She doesn't seem as old as my friends' grandmothers. She makes me feel happy. I can't wait to get to England. Will we have time to sight-see? I hope Dancer has a good trip. He's never done this before. Neither have I! Do you get sick in planes, Mom? I hope I don't. I wonder if the royal family is nice. Do you think we'll get to meet them? I mean, personally?' And so it went.

They arrived in lots of time and parked the truck and trailer at the previously designated meeting place behind the terminal buildings. The Brigadier had arranged that the groom, George, who'd be travelling with them, would be waiting there. A small man wearing a green plaid cap smiled and waved as they turned in.

'That must be George,' chirped Mousie, who hadn't stopped talking since they'd left Hogscroft.

George helped them unload Dancer. Dancer snorted, and sniffed at him. Very gently, as Mousie held him, George stroked first his nose, and then his neck as he talked softly. Mousie and Christine could see that he was a man with a great love of horses, and that put their minds completely at rest. Dancer seemed to think so, too, because he walked off with the groom like a gentleman. Their fears about Dancer misbehaving with a stranger were allayed.

'Did you see that?' asked Christine. 'Not a fuss. George certainly knows horses.'

'Well, we introduced them properly. And he doesn't seem to mind as long as I hand the reins over. Then he understands.'

Christine shook her head. 'He's a complicated animal.'

'Have a good trip, Dancer,' Mousie called, watching him go. Dancer whinnied and looked back at them. 'You, too,' he seemed to say.

Just then, another man walked up to them.

'Hello, Mrs James and Hilary. I'm Hugh Allen. I'll be looking after your every need; arranging seats and organizing every detail. I'm pleased to be of service. Just lock up your rig, and we'll drive over to the terminal in my car.'

They were there in no time. He smiled as he took their passports and luggage, and ushered them into the first-class lounge.

'It wouldn't be so bad to live like this,' Mousie gasped as they sank into the comfortable chairs in the lounge. 'Don't you feel spoiled?'

'Would you like a coffee, orange juice, wine, a drink, anything?' Mr Allen asked them. 'There are cookies or cheese and crackers. Can I get you something before I go to finalize things?'

'Thank you, Mr Allen, but you go ahead. Hilary and I will

look after ourselves.' Christine smiled her thanks.

'Excellent. I'll be back presently.'

Mr Allen left the lounge and Mousie said, 'Doesn't he have a glorious English accent?'

'Get used to it, Mousie.'

'This is so much fun! Did you realize that you called me Hilary to Mr Allen?'

'Well, you don't look like a Mousie all dressed up like that. You're so grown up.'

'I'm almost seventeen, Mom. You were just a few years older than me when you got married.'

'Four years older. Almost five. But you're right.'

'They're sure looking after us. A groom, a keeper, first-class seats, and Dancer's flying on the same plane as us.'

Christine smiled warmly and squeezed her daughter's hand. She enjoyed Mousie's enthusiasm.

The flight took off on time. Mousie and Christine sat in the spacious seats at the front of the plane. They were to be served a four-course meal with wine, then a movie would be shown.

'I'd recommend that we try to sleep instead of watching the film, honey,' said Christine.

'You're no fun, it's *The Kronos Syndrome*! I don't see why I can't watch just a little of it.'

'Trust me. If you watch a little, you'll want to see how it ends.'

'So what? Why can't I enjoy every bit of this trip if I want to?'

'Suit yourself, but I'm sleeping. Don't keep me awake.'

'Spoilsport,' Mousie muttered under her breath.

'I heard that.'

They eventually got a little sleep, Christine more than Mousie, and the trip was uneventful and smooth. They landed at Heathrow on time, feeling eager for the adventure, but very tired. They were met by another 'keeper', this time a woman named Caroline.

'Welcome to England, Mrs James, Hilary. I hope you had a good flight.' She smiled graciously at them. 'Percy, your driver, is waiting outside with your limousine.' She waved her hand in the direction of the exit. 'We've arranged accommodation at "Clusters", a lovely country home that's recently been converted to a small but very comfortable hotel. If you wish, we'll go there directly so that you can rest and freshen up.' She looked at Mousie. 'Your horse will go on to Highgrove in a horse-box with George.' Caroline motioned toward some comfortable chairs. 'If you would be so kind as to have a seat in the lobby, I'll arrange for your luggage.'

'Mom, they're treating us like royalty!' Mousie couldn't believe this.

'We certainly can't complain.' Christine smiled, thoroughly enjoying herself.

'I just wish I'd been able to get more sleep on the plane,' grumbled Mousie.

Christine gave her a jab in the ribs.

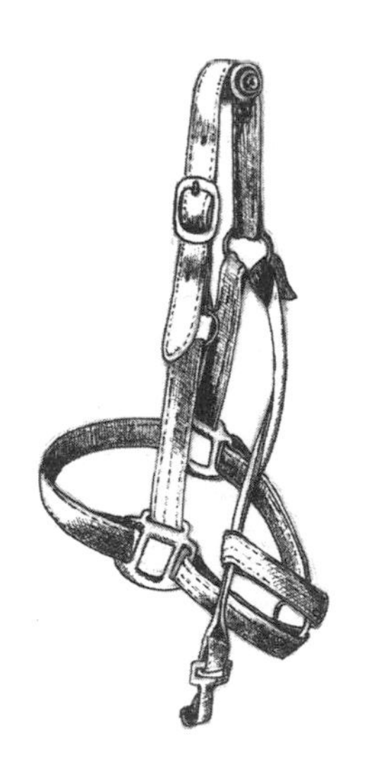

Chapter 7

Arabella

THEIR DESTINATION WAS a village near Highgrove, called Tetbury. The changing scenery kept their attention riveted as the powerful limousine whisked them through the streets. They gaped at the sights of London, vigorous and bustling, then the suburbs, green, tranquil and inviting. Just past Swindon the driver turned off the M4 and they found themselves in the Cotswold countryside.

They felt they'd entered an enchanted world. They gazed through the car windows as they passed through Callow Hill, Malmesbury, and Long Newton. The landscapes were marvellous to see; the green hills, meandering streams, gracious trees and cosy stone houses with crumbling stone walls. The winding roads were sunk deep into the earth and sometimes weren't wide enough for two cars to pass.

After being in the 'motor' for about two hours, they reached Tetbury. Such a pleasant little place, Christine thought to herself. It certainly wouldn't be a bad way to live. They pulled up in front of a charming ivy-covered limestone Georgian mansion. There were wings on either side of the main house; a handsome square building with a stately portico and many large inviting windows.

'We're staying here?' Mousie asked her mother incredulously.

'Looks like it,' Christine answered happily.

They stepped out of the car and took a good look. The mansion was set a long way back from the road, the driveway cutting straight through a small park before ending in a circle at the gardens by the front. It seemed as though the parkland continued far behind the Georgian house, but they'd have to check that out later.

They were greeted by a tall, serious-looking man who nodded to the driver and invited them to enter.

The dour manservant carried their luggage, leading them through the entrance hall to their rooms. He talked expressionlessly as he showed them the way.

'Clusters was built in 1743 by the fourth Duke of Dewbury. He was Master of the Hounds and outlived three wives. Two of them were killed in fox-hunting accidents. You're staying in the suite of his second wife, Arabella. We've maintained her taste in decor, to keep her ghost happy.' Mousie gasped and put her hand to her mouth. His mouth twitched briefly when he saw that his story had elicited the desired effect. 'Arabella was kind and delightful. No reason why her ghost would want to harm you. She loved horses, and it's said that she could do things with them that no one else could. Some say she could talk their language.'

'How did she die?' Mousie whispered, not sure she really wanted to know.

The manservant squinted at her, and replied with morbid relish, 'Her mount collided with an enormous black horse in mid-flight, jumping over a stone wall. Her favourite bay hunter slipped in the mud as he tried to right himself, and they crashed over backwards, smashing to the ground. They say the horse flipped back, right on top of her, and broke her back and neck. The hunt continued. Tally ho. No one bothered to see if they could help. They say the horse wouldn't leave her side. He died of a broken heart.' He paused, for effect. 'Well, I must take my leave. Ring if there's anything at all.' The manservant left the room, quite pleased at the impression he'd made.

Mousie swallowed, wide-eyed. 'Wow, Mom. What a romantic story. I wish I could've met Arabella.'

She looked around Arabella's room. It was all in white and blue. The wallpaper and the fabric of the floor-length drapes were matched; periwinkle-blue hunt scenes on a white background. The beds were covered in embroidered white linen with bedskirts and bolsters of the same. There were antique carpets in faded blues and whites and reds and greens on the polished oak floor. Bright red tulips in a blue and white ceramic vase were placed on the highly polished oak table beside the fireplace. Sunshine streamed in from the large multi-paned windows overlooking the spacious, well-tended grounds.

'Mom, this is totally incredible. One day if I'm ever rich I'll decorate my bedroom just like this.'

They unpacked their clothes and put them in the drawers of the huge, gleaming oak armoire.

'Look, Mom!' Mousie gasped as she opened a drawer. She carefully lifted out an antique wooden whip bound in aged leather. There was a beautifully shaped silver horse-leg at the end, knee bent in a trotting position. That end was used to hook onto latches to open gates, or to pick things up off the ground. At the other end was a long, braided leather tail, for snapping at the hounds to gather them. 'A lady's hunting whip! I bet it belonged to Arabella!'

'What an imagination you have, Mousie! The fellow was just trying to give us a dash of ghostly English history. With quite a flair, I might add.' Christine shook her head, chuckling. This was going to be fun.

After a short but refreshing nap, Christine and Mousie showered and dressed for their tour of the Highgrove stables and then dinner with Caroline at the Wheatsheaf. They chose their mid-calf skirts with boots and jackets. For good measure, they tied silk scarves creatively around their necks.

'Thank God for your gran!' exclaimed Christine as she admired herself in the mirror. They knew they looked just right, and felt giddy with expectation. Mousie pinched herself to make sure it was all real.

Percy the chauffeur was waiting in the lobby with Caroline, and they stood as the two women walked down the sweeping staircase.

'Are we ready to go, madam?' the elderly driver asked.

'Absolutely!' Mousie chirped. The old man twinkled at her youthful enthusiasm, and held open the door.

It was evening and the dusky sky was alight with pinks and purples. They drove on a winding road with tall hedges on either side. There were glimpses of rolling fields through the partings in the hedges. In less than five minutes they turned into the Highgrove stables.

Mousie and Christine got out of the car and looked around. They were in a cobbled courtyard surrounded by old stone stables in mint condition. Each stall faced the centre of the courtyard; each had a door divided in half horizontally. The bottom doors were closed, and with the top doors open, the horses could all look out. Mousie grabbed her mother by the arm, awed. 'This is out of a movie, Mom.'

'I'll wait here, madam and miss. Take your time.' Percy had taken a liking to Mousie, and he gave her a private little thumbs-up sign.

'Dancer!' Christine gasped. The athletic horse had drawn back on his haunches, tucked his head to his forelegs, and leapt over the four-foot door of his stall when he saw who had arrived. Sparks flew in every direction as his steel shoes struck the stones. The air smelled as if a hundred matches had been lit. He looked astonished at the effect, but in a stride or two he was by their side, nuzzling and nickering.

'Dancer, you wonderful animal,' Mousie said, rubbing his face and hugging him. 'What will they think of you, jumping out like that?'

'Not so much at the moment, if you don't mind me saying.' A small harassed-looking man in his thirties hurried up to

Dancer and tried to grab him by the halter. The horse reared up to avoid contact. 'I'm doing my best, I really am, but this is one trouble-maker. He won't stay in his stall if we leave the top open, and if we close it, he kicks the stall in.'

'Eddie,' Caroline reprimanded him. 'These people have come here all the way from Canada. Please extend some courtesy.'

'Yes, ma'am. I'm sorry, ma'am. It's just that we've got ten new horses here for the show, and no new staff, and he's making things difficult for us.'

'Dancer does need special care, that's true. You have to treat him almost like you'd treat a human, or he gets upset.' Christine tried to speak in a calming voice, hiding her concern. 'But we don't need to keep him here if you think he's too much trouble. Perhaps there are stables nearby that you'd recommend.'

'Now I'm not saying that I can't handle him, ma'am. I just need to get used to him. And there's not a stable around that could do a better job.'

Mousie tried earnestly to explain. 'What my mother is trying to say is that Dancer's more difficult than most horses until you get to know him, and then he's fine. So, if you have too many horses to look after, it'd be much better for him if he went somewhere else.'

'I think it'll all work out fine.' Eddie tried to smile sincerely, but Mousie wasn't satisfied.

'Do you want me to stay and help you with him?' she asked.

'You already have helped by explaining his personality. Much appreciated.' Eddie touched his hand to his cap and nodded. 'I look forward to caring for such a talented horse.' He went on his way.

Sensing their concern, Caroline said, 'I'd like to introduce you to Morgan, our head groom. He's in charge of the whole operation and he'll be here at all times.'

'Thanks, Caroline,' answered Christine. 'I'd feel much better if Eddie had some help with Dancer.' Mousie quickly nodded her agreement. Dancer snorted.

'Done. Give me one minute.' Caroline left them with Dancer, in the courtyard, as she went to find Morgan.

'Dancer, what have you been up to?' Mousie hugged him fiercely. They walked back to the stall from where he'd jumped, and put him in. 'I'd hate to have to close you in, Dancer, but it's not like home. People expect you to act like an ordinary horse. If you jump out, they'll have to close the top door.' As usual, Dancer seemed to understand all that Mousie said. He settled calmly into his stall, munching hay, as Caroline reappeared.

'We're so very sorry about this, Hilary, Mrs James. Eddie's our best groom. He's an excellent horseman, and we've never had a problem with him since he stopped gambling. But that was long ago. I shouldn't even have mentioned it. Please forgive me.' She smiled sheepishly, embarrassed that she'd been indiscreet. 'The head groom, Morgan, will take a personal interest in Dancer. He's on his way now to meet you.'

'Thank you so much,' Christine smiled warmly at the woman. 'Don't worry, everything will be fine.'

They met Morgan, a strong, confident man in his thirties, and discussed the care of Dancer. They were satisfied that he was in very good hands.

When the horse was cared for and bedded down, Caroline, Mousie and Christine returned to the limousine and were driven to the pub in the middle of town.

The main rooms of the Wheatsheaf were panelled with rich oak, and candles glowed from every table. The mood was low-key and cheerful, and they had a hearty dinner of potatoes and roast beef with gravy. Plans were discussed for the next day and time-tables for the show gone over.

As they drove back to Clusters, Mousie and Christine felt well organized and very well fed. They also were getting to know Caroline a little better, and warmed to her gentle, considerate ways.

'Do you think I'd be able to go on a hunt while I'm here?' Mousie asked Caroline as she was getting out of the limousine.

She was startled. 'Fox-hunt? Let me enquire. It's considered to be quite dangerous for the uninitiated, you know.'

'Well, it's just a thought. Forget it if it's any trouble. Really.'

'Let me discuss it with the organizers of the show. Were you thinking of hunting Dancer?'

'Yes. He'd really love it.'

'Do you hunt him in Canada?'

'We haven't yet, but that's a great idea.'

'Well, if he's never been hunted, perhaps it would be better if you rode an experienced hunter. Some horses get too excited.'

'Hilary,' Christine interrupted. 'The horse show's tomorrow. Why don't you get it behind you before making plans to hunt.'

'Very sensible, madam,' said a relieved Caroline, 'but I'll make enquiries in the event that you'd like to go.'

They said their good-nights to Caroline and Percy, and planned to meet in the morning at eight-thirty, after breakfast.

Mousie and Christine were so tired that they hardly spoke to each other. They washed, brushed their teeth, and got into their flannel nighties in record time. They climbed into the duvet-covered feather beds, Mousie giggling with joy, and snuggled into the cosy mattresses. Sleep came immediately.

Mousie was dreaming. A beautiful blonde woman riding side-saddle, was galloping across a barren, windswept plain. The sky was dark and stormy. Her long black hunting gown was torn, her white blouse and stock-tie wet and splattered with mud. The veil that had been attached to her riding hat was ripped, and was flapping in the wind. Blood trickled down her face. Her dark bay hunter was tired, labouring hard. His sides were heaving, his coat lathered with sweat. Lightning flashed. Thunder crashed. She slowly turned to look at Mousie. Her eyes were hollow and serious, her words urgent. 'Go ... to ... Dancer.' Mousie couldn't hear her, the wind was howling so loudly. She read her lips. 'Go ... to ... Dancer.' The woman was calling out to her, straining to be heard. 'Go ... to ... Dancer.'

Mousie sat straight up in bed. It was dark. The clock read four-thirty. That woman in my dream. She's been in my dreams before. The night Chad Smith died. Dancer needs me, she thought.

She quietly pulled on her sweat-suit and running shoes, and left the room. She tiptoed down the darkened hall and down the stairs, through the foyer, and out the stately front door. There's only one thing to do, she thought, and that's to find out if there's anything wrong. She knew she'd never get back to sleep, anyway.

Running as fast as she dared, she stumbled on a clod of earth and righted herself. She tripped over some branches at the side of the road. She trusted that she was going the right way. This is crazy, she thought, but what if he's in trouble? He's been in trouble often enough, she mused. She ran faster.

Ten or fifteen minutes later she could see the stables on the left just a little way off. There weren't any lights on, and Mousie gave serious thought to turning back. She could get herself arrested entering private property at such an odd hour. And it was just a dream. How stupid can I get, she thought. But since she was already so near, she decided to pay Dancer a visit. And she had to be sure.

As she crept into the courtyard after climbing the gate, she was convinced that she'd let her imagination carry her away. She peeked over the half-door into his stall, fully expecting to see her sleeping horse. It was empty. Dancer was gone.

What should she do? Where should she look? She looked around. There was nothing but darkness. It was very difficult to see. There was a little glow of white light over by the arch leading to the arena.

Down the cobblestone hallway she went toward the light. She heard scraping and scuffling noises. 'Dancer!' she called out. There was a frantic whinny in response. Mousie flew. She turned to the left, following the noise, and came upon a horrible sight.

Dancer was held by a rope, one end at his halter, the other wrapped around his rump. He was covered in sweat, raw with rope burns and blood was dripping down his back leg. Eddie was struggling, straining against Dancer's weight, holding on to the rope with all his strength.

'What's going on?' Mousie demanded.

Eddie dropped the rope, startled, and Dancer scrambled for his balance. 'He escaped again,' stammered Eddie. 'I thought he was going to run away, so I roped him. He wouldn't come quietly. He was fighting me, and we've been having a tussle. I daren't let him go, I thought he'd kill me.'

By now, Mousie was at Dancer's side, and could see that he was exhausted. He relaxed visibly and nudged her gratefully with his nose. She could only guess how long this had been going on. She took a deep breath to control her temper, but her anger was apparent.

'Eddie, I told you already,' she said through clenched teeth. 'You have to talk to him, and tell him what you're doing. Otherwise he gets scared and he fights.' She turned abruptly and walked away. Eddie stood there staring after them as Dancer followed Mousie like a puppy back to his stall without a lead-line.

Once back at his stall, she examined her horse. He'd be fine, she was relieved to see. The rope burns were superficial. They would heal well. There was a slash on his back left rump. It looked like he'd bashed into the wall and scraped himself on a nail. That, too, would heal up before long. She washed him down, applied balm and talked to him, vowing never to leave his side. She stayed with him until a boy came with his morning feed.

'What time is it?'

'Half past five, Miss.'

'Is Morgan here yet?'

'Yes, Miss, everyone's here by now.'

'Would you please tell him that I need to speak with him as soon as possible.' Mousie tried to handle this with calmness. The stable boy rushed off.

Morgan arrived only minutes later. Mousie told him what had happened, being careful to underline that it wasn't totally Eddie's fault. Faced with a loose, unco-operative horse, many people might've done a similar thing. Morgan took a look at Dancer's injuries, and angrily went in pursuit of Eddie.

Mousie called to the boy, 'Could you come here, please?' The boy approached nervously. He'd heard rumours of what had gone on from the other boys, and didn't want any trouble.

'I need to make a call. Can you tell me where the phone is?'

'There's a telephone right here, over the bales of hay.'

Mousie thanked him gratefully, and walked the few paces to where the phone was hanging, masked behind some cooling blankets.

The boy called Clusters, and when he got through he handed her the phone. She asked to speak to Christine James. While she waited for her mother to get on the line, she glanced at her watch. It was almost six o'clock. She hoped her mother would be awake.

'Hello?' answered Christine, her voice filled with anxiety.

'Mom! It's me. I'm at the stables.'

'Mousie! Thank goodness you called! I didn't know where you were. I just woke up and you were gone. Is everything all right?'

'Everything's fine now, Mom. Dancer jumped out during the night and was looking around, and Eddie, remember, the groom? lassoed him and they had a rumble, so Dancer's got rope burns and a gash where he probably knocked into the wall. I don't think Eddie meant any harm, but I still don't like it one bit. Dancer's all upset, so I don't want to leave. Do you think you could bring me some clothes and something to eat? I'm in my track-suit. Oh, and bring my show clothes, too.'

'I'll call Percy now, and I'll be there as soon as possible. What made you go over there in the first place?'

'I had a ... I'll tell you later. It sounds silly.'

'Well, I'm glad you're all right. I'm glad you called. I didn't know what to think.'

'Thanks, Mom. See you later.'

'I'll be there soon. Bye, sweetie.'

Mousie went back to Dancer's stall. He put his head over her shoulder. She encircled his neck in her arms and they stood together peacefully until Dancer was sound asleep. He was calm with Mousie there with him. She lay down on the straw, and dozed off.

Mousie awoke to the sound of her mother gently calling to her. 'Mousie, honey, wake up, it's nine-fifteen.'

Mousie leapt up. Her practice started in a little over half an hour. She checked on Dancer, who was wide awake, munching on hay and looking his old self.

'Mom, I'm sorry I scared you.'

'I'm glad that everything's okay, Mousie. But maybe next time you could leave a note.' She smiled at her daughter and shook her head, remembering her panic upon awakening to an empty bed and Mousie nowhere in sight.

After Mousie's call, Christine had come directly to the stables, and finding her daughter asleep, had sought out Morgan. He assured her that everything was in order. They were short-staffed with all the extra horses, but Eddie would be sent home after his shift was over, where he would remain until his situation was reviewed.

Christine didn't want to alarm Mousie, but she had an uneasy feeling about the night's events. She felt strongly that Eddie wasn't to be trusted, although she had no real reason. She wasn't ready to excuse him.

'Have some breakfast, honey.' Christine produced a tempting array of food, prepared in a hurry by Clusters' kitchen. There was a bacon sandwich, freshly squeezed orange juice, and a sugary Danish pastry. Mousie devoured it all, then let Dancer lick the sugar off her fingers.

She went off to change into her old riding clothes for the practice. Her show clothes were in the suitcase, clean and ready for the show, which would be starting at four o'clock that afternoon. Christine stayed with Dancer so he wouldn't jump out, just for Mousie's peace of mind.

The practice was set up so that the ten riders could all get to know each other and warm up their horses. There'd be a lunch for the contestants afterwards.

Mousie had a great time at the practice, the events of the early morning temporarily forgotten. Christine watched from the stands, and reflected on how wonderful it was for her daughter to have been given this unusual invitation. It was an experience that she'd never forget.

When it came time for the competitors' lunch, Christine contentedly settled inside Dancer's stall with a lawn-chair and a good book. She'd insisted that she'd be happier there with Dancer. Mousie went off surrounded by her new-found friends, and Dancer promptly lay down and slept. Time passed peacefully for Christine.

She was deep into her book, when she overheard someone softly approaching the telephone beside Dancer's stall.

'Collect call to Canada,' a voice said. Christine couldn't help overhearing, though it was in such low, rushed tones that she couldn't hear the phone number given. 'And hurry.'

Christine strained to hear and prayed that she was totally out of sight in the stall. She wanted to take a look at who was speaking in such a furtive way, but she dared not move.

'It's me, Eddie. No luck .... The girl came before I could get him out.... No one was here. It was early enough!... Yeah, a scratch or two. The bastard was stubborn as a mule. He wouldn't budge! ... Look, I gotta go.... Yeah, I got the first half but it's a tougher job than you said. I'll want another five hundred quid.... Uh, what?... For four thou? ... You gotta be kidding.... No.... It's ten and nothing less.... You got a deal.... Right.... I'll get it done.... Right.'

Christine sat deathly still as the groom walked to Dancer's stall. He studied the sleeping horse silently, inches from Christine. Christine thought he must surely see her. Suddenly, he moved off. She slowly let out her breath and contemplated what to do.

Mousie returned with a sandwich and coffee for her mother. She braided Dancer's mane and tail and chattered to her mother about the kids and who said what. She picked out his feet, painted them with pine tar and neatsfoot oil, polished the tack, groomed her horse within an inch of his life, and even brushed his teeth. Dancer was definitely ready. At three-thirty, after tacking him up, Mousie went to change, bubbling with excitement.

She returned, her face puzzled. 'Mom, why'd you pack Arabella's hunting whip?'

'I didn't.' Christine looked at Mousie, who was holding up the antique whip that she'd found in the drawer at Clusters.

'You must've, because it was in the suitcase with my things.'

'Well, I didn't intend to, Mousie. I don't know how it got there.'

They didn't discuss it further, because Morgan came to inform them that the royal family had assembled for the show. Mousie nimbly mounted Dancer and waved goodbye to her mother.

'Good luck, honey. I'll be watching.'

'Thanks, Mom.' She suddenly stopped.

'Anything wrong?' Christine tensed, sure that Mousie had sensed her unease about Eddie.

'No. But why don't I ride with Arabella's hunting whip? She was a great horsewoman. Who knows, it might bring me luck!'

Christine, relieved, handed it to her. It felt warm in her hand. Strange, she thought. Must've been beside the heater.

'See you later, Mom!' Mousie walked Dancer through the hall to the warm-up ring, adjacent to the big arena where the jumps were set up for the show.

This competition was to be judged on time as well as faults, and the riders were tense. She tried to relax and forget that the royal family was sitting just beyond those doors. The hunting whip felt strangely comforting in her grip, even though she'd never ridden with one before. She was issued her favourite number, seven, which was also her placement in the line-up. Mousie remained calm, putting her faith in Dancer.

Christine sat in the stands reserved for friends and family of the riders. She couldn't put Eddie's secret phone call out of her mind. The foreboding kept creeping back. Eddie would be sent home very soon, so perhaps she had nothing to worry about. But what about the money? What was that about? And why was he calling Canada? More to the point, who was he calling? Should she confide in Morgan? She wasn't sure what to do. For the moment, all she could do was try to concentrate on the show.

From where she sat she had a good view, not only of the arena, but of the royal family. The Queen was seated in the center of the front row, her playful corgis on either side. She was comfortably dressed in a tweed skirt and jacket. Her husband, Prince Philip, was on her right, and Prince Charles sat on her left. Princess Anne, Princess Margaret, Prince Andrew, Prince Edward with a new girlfriend, the six royal grandchildren and some of the less well-known royals were seated all around the Queen. Altogether, with the important-looking invited guests, there were about seventy spectators.

The show began. The first rider, a freckled young man with shocking red hair, rode in on a muscled bay. Christine thought it might be a Hanoverian cross. He did very well over the tricky course, knocking down only one rail, and making nice time. There was enthusiastic applause, and the next rider appeared, riding a nervous, high-stepping grey.

Christine had attended many horse shows in her life. She'd competed herself, many years before, as Joy sat patiently through countless competitions. She'd never done as well as Mousie. She'd had neither the horse nor the remarkable talent. Mousie and Dancer had gone all the way through the little summer fairs, the large shows, and then the Royal Winter Fair. Christine smiled as she reflected on the years of work and love that her family had put into this demanding sport.

Mousie rode into the arena, the seventh competitor. Dancer was showing off and enjoying every minute; high-stepping in his loose-limbed, muscular way, with his head tucked and his neck arched. The crowd loved him. Christine saw the Queen whisper something into Charles's ear, then into Philip's. Mousie looked splendid, her silky hair braided down her back, holding the silver-footed hunting whip. Dancer was in top form, his glossy chestnut coat warmly reflecting the light. From the stands, Christine could hardly see the gash on his leg.

Although these horses and riders were hand-picked by the Queen for their expertise in the show ring, there had been only two clear rounds up until now, both with somewhat slowish times. It occurred to Christine that the course was difficult, and the contestants might be suffering, understandably, from nerves. Mousie, however, looked radiant and as cool as a cucumber. Christine was amazed at her daughter's aplomb. Usually she was a bundle of nerves.

Dancer and Mousie joyfully sailed together over high rails and tricky in-and-outs, over wide water hazards and colourful barrels. Not a rail was so much as rapped. They had an exceptionally fast time, and did it with such ease that the course looked simple. They left the arena to the biggest applause of the afternoon.

The three remaining riders had good rounds, but a couple of rails had been knocked down and none finished with as fast a time as Dancer's. Mousie was the winner.

For the amusement of the royal party, Dancer and Mousie were invited to take the course again, over raised bars. They soared over everything in sight once again, delighting and astounding the audience with their seamless performance.

Elizabeth herself rose in her chair, and beckoned Mousie. Mousie rode Dancer to the enclosure and stopped, facing the Queen.

'My dear, well done. We were so sorry to have witnessed your terrible fall in Canada. We're very happy that you've fully recovered. You are a remarkable rider, and my dear, you have a most remarkable horse.' She smiled at her and then sat.

Mousie couldn't say a word. She was flabbergasted. She was happy and grateful and dazed. The Queen of England had spoken to her! Just as she unlocked her mouth to say thank you, Dancer reared up and held his position for five seconds, nostrils flaring and ears pricked. He dropped to the ground, bowed deeply, then spun around and trotted out.

There wasn't a sound in the stands for a few seconds. Such a show of magnificence was truly rare, and the small audience began to acknowledge it with quiet, awed applause, cascading into a standing ovation.

Mousie and Christine were thrilled with Dancer's performance. They tended to him after the show, and took extra care with his bruises and cuts. They left Highgrove after cleaning, feeding, and heaping lavish praise on his deserving ears. They were assured by Morgan that Eddie was at home with his sister and that a stable boy would be on guard at all times. Christine, secure in the knowledge that Morgan was in control of the situation, decided not to alarm Mousie by telling her about the phone call she had overheard. There seemed no point.

Percy, the kind chauffeur, let them out at the front door of Clusters. He reminded them that he'd be back at eight-fifteen to take them to the closing dinner.

Still flushed with Mousie's success, the ladies walked through the elegant entrance hall and up the grand staircase toward their suite. The manservant carried the suitcase. It occurred to Mousie that it seemed days since she'd crept out, anxious about her dream. It couldn't possibly have been only that same morning.

Along the upstairs hall were hung large, gilt-framed, ancient oil portraits of aristocratic-looking men and women. Some stood proudly, gazing out, or sat up stiffly in formal settings, dressed in the finery of the day. Others had more relaxed poses, playing with puppies or smiling with children. The colours were rich, but muted with the passing years. Mousie glanced at them as she walked along, thinking about how much family history they represented. She considered asking her mother to get one painted of herself and Dancer. When they got rich, she chuckled to herself.

Suddenly she stopped, transfixed. She gaped at a painting of a blonde woman, kind-looking and beautiful, dressed in a black flowing riding habit with a veil, sitting sidesaddle on a handsome bay hunter.

'Who's this?' she croaked.

'Why that's Miss Arabella, the second wife of the Duke of Dewbury. You're staying in her room.'

'Mousie, what's wrong?' Christine looked with concern at her daughter, who'd gone completely white.

'Was this picture hanging here yesterday?' she demanded of the manservant.

'No, miss. It's been away being cleaned. I rehung it only this morning.'

It had been Arabella, the second wife of the Duke of Dewbury, killed in a hunting accident, who'd warned her when Dancer was in trouble. Twice. Mousie fell to the floor in a dead faint.

Chapter 8

Cassandra

MOUSIE CAME TO, tucked into her feather bed. Her mother was sitting in a chair beside the bed.

'Mousie. Hello. How about a cup of good English tea?'

'Hi, Mom. How long have I been sleeping?'

'About half an hour. A perfect beauty nap. I've run the bath for you.'

'Great.'

'How do you feel?'

'Much better, thanks.'

'Do you want to tell me why you passed out?'

Mousie paused. 'Can I tell you while we're having tea? Tea sounds just right.'

Christine nodded and picked up the phone to order tea for two. Mousie had a luxurious soak in the tub while they waited for it to arrive. Christine put her feet up and thought about Eddie's call. She was deliberating on exactly what to do, and Mousie was cosily wrapped in her terrytowel robe when there was a knock on the door.

'Thank you so much,' Christine said to the manservant, as he wheeled in delicious-looking scones with butter and an assortment of jams along with a beautiful porcelain teapot and cups.

'My pleasure, madam. And I've been asked to tell you that you had a call from Canada while you were out. Here is the number.'

'Thank you,' Christine signed the bill, and the manservant left the room, nodding his head in a slight bow.

'This is our number. Your gran must have called. I hope nothing's wrong.'

'She might just be wondering how we're doing, Mom,' Mousie reassured her mother.

'Hmm. It's seven in the evening here. What time is it in Canada?'

'Subtract five hours, and you get, uh, two in the afternoon. Is that right?'

'Right. I hope she's home. It might be urgent.' Christine dreaded that it might be. She put in the call and waited only a few seconds for Joy to answer.

'Hello?'

'Mom, it's Christine. Is everything okay?'

'Everything's fine. I just had to share some gossip.'

'You called me in England to share some gossip, Mom? I was worried!'

'This concerns you, dear, otherwise I wouldn't have bothered,' she chuckled across the Atlantic Ocean. 'You'll find it very interesting, so don't take my head off.'

'Go on, tell me.'

'Rory Casey came to see me this morning.'

'Rory came to see you?' Christine's heart started to beat faster.

'His wife, Helena, has finally agreed to a divorce. He's desperate that you know. He's far more handsome than I remember, Christine, so distinguished-looking with his silver hair. I promised him that I'd try to get through. Christine, are you there? Christine, you haven't said a word!'

'Mom, I'm trying to absorb this. I don't know what to say. I feel numb.'

'Do you want to know why he couldn't call you himself?'

'Why?'

'Because he and Sandy are trying to get a flight to England.'

'They're what? Now? You're joking!'

'Trust me, my dear, I wouldn't joke about something like this.'

'When will they be here? Does he know where we are?'

'I don't know which flight they'll be able to catch at such short notice, so I don't know when they'll be there. But yes, I told him how to find you.'

'Mom, this is amazing.'

'I've been waiting for your call. Now I'm off to meet the girls, but let me give you one piece of advice.' Joy paused for effect. 'You're not getting any younger.'

'You're awful, Mom! Goodbye!' Christine chuckled as she hung up, her mother's gales of laughter crackling down the line.

Mousie had been standing next to Christine and heard the whole conversation. She threw her arms around her mother.

'Mom, I'm so happy for you! Will you marry him?'

'Don't put the cart before the horse. We haven't even dated! Honey, there's a lot to think about. I'm not going to rush into anything.'

'But you love him, don't you? And I know he loves you.'

'You're such a romantic, Mousie! Rory and I have to get to know each other all over again. Let's just see how things go. But I must admit, this news sure makes me feel happy!'

It was time to dress for dinner, and the two women went about their tasks, each preoccupied by her own thoughts. Christine was thinking about a possible future with Rory, and Mousie was mulling over Sandy's surprise arrival in England. Thoughts of Eddie and Arabella were pushed aside, and the tea sat untouched.

Christine and Mousie arrived at Highgrove feeling as if they were characters in a fairy tale. The stone walls of the vast arena adjoining the stables were lit with burning torches, recalling knights in armour and damsels in distress. The young grooms were dressed in blue velvet livery and were acting as ushers, graciously guiding the delighted guests into the festively decorated arena, where only that afternoon, the jumps had stood. Mousie and Christine admired the horseshoe-shaped wreaths of flowers on the walls and the colourful centrepieces on the tables, with rose buds, daisies, and violets pouring out of tipped urns. The tables were set handsomely, and the delicious aromas of dinner made their mouths water.

An energetic, smiling young groom approached them. He bowed his head slightly, then spoke.

'I have been given the honour of escorting you to your table tonight. I'm rather pleased to meet the young Canadian rider who showed us how it's done.' He looked shyly at Mousie. 'Oh, and her mother too.'

Mousie grinned at Christine, and answered, 'Enchanted, I'm sure,' and stifled a giggle. The groom blushed, and said, 'Her Majesty is at Dancer's stall. She requests a word with you before you go in. I'll take you directly to her.'

Mousie and Christine looked at each other in astonishment. They followed him, Christine full of silent questions and Mousie eager. The groom chatted nervously as they walked, unable to bear silence.

'Her Majesty is rather taken with your horse. I've rarely seen her like this. She loves her corgis, you know, makes a real fuss over them. And she has some really rather top-notch horses. But when she went to Canada in the fall, she was rather impressed by your horse Dancer, and wanted to invite you here so she could show him off to her family. I wasn't picked to go on that trip, even though they were scouting out new lines for breeding. Mr Morgan chose Eddie. Well, here we are. It was a pleasure meeting you.' The young man gave Mousie a quick admiring glance, then took his leave.

Christine and Mousie approached the Queen. She looked smaller than they'd imagined, and certainly more like a real person than a queen. She was wearing a simple, well-tailored dinner dress, with a matching jacket, and sensible shoes.

She'd have no idea that a groom in her stables is on the take, Christine thought. She'd be horrified. Christine also wondered if Eddie was at home where he was supposed to be.

Two corgis were playing beside the Queen, jumping up to sniff Dancer's nose as he snorted. This was a game he played with Pepper at home.

'Please come and stand closer. You're Hilary,' Queen Elizabeth smiled at Mousie, 'and you are her mother, Mrs James?'

'Yes, Your Majesty.' Christine curtsied, and Mousie copied her, awkwardly.

'We're so pleased you were able to visit. Are you having a pleasant time?'

'Just wonderful, Your Royal Highness!' gushed Mousie, then clapped her hand over her mouth remembering too late that the Queen is always 'Your Majesty'. Her husband and children – mere princes and princessess – are to be addressed as 'Your Royal Highness'.

The Queen, appearing not to notice Mousie's gaffe, continued, 'We have made no secret of our admiration for Dancer, and we are currently in need of a horse to take the place of Centennial, our favourite. He was a gift from your country, you know, and he died quite a few years ago.' She shook her head, sadly. 'We've never replaced him, and until we saw Daring Dancer, we didn't think too much about it. There's no shortage of horses, as you see.' The Queen looked intently at Mousie. 'We were hoping that if you were ever considering a change of home for Dancer, you would contact us directly.'

Mousie stood for a moment, stunned. Then she spoke.

'Ma'am, I'm terribly complimented.' Mousie was nervous. She swallowed. 'But Dancer's much more than a horse to me. He's my best friend. He came to our farm soon after my dad died. He helped me to, well, want to live again. I talk to him about everything, and he understands.' Mousie had tears in her eyes. 'Nothing can ever take my dad's place, Your Majesty, but Dancer helps.'

The Queen was moved. She looked kindly at Mousie. 'Hilary, I understand. Perhaps this explains the connection, almost the magic, between the two of you. Perhaps he wouldn't even be happy with me.'

'I'm sure he'd be happy here, Ma'am. But my daughter would be very sad to lose Dancer.' Christine put her arm around Mousie's shoulders.

Elizabeth brightened. 'He is entire, isn't he? Is he a stallion?'

'Yes,' answered Christine.

'Lovely. We have a proposal. May we have the honour of a breeding? Our lovely mare Cassandra is ready to be mated. It would be the perfect solution.'

Dancer seemed to be listening. His eyes were bright, his ears pricked, and he nickered.

'Dancer thinks that's a fine idea,' laughed Mousie. 'Okay!'

'Splendid.' The Queen was pleased.

'Can we meet Cassandra?' asked Mousie.

'She's at the stud's now. Morgan!' she called. Morgan came from down the hall and bowed his head to the Queen, and then nodded to Christine and Mousie. 'Telephone over to the stud's immediately and cancel Cassandra's breeding. Have her delivered here early tomorrow.' She turned back to Christine and Mousie. 'You'll be able to see her tomorrow morning. Come at ten o'clock and she'll be here. We're delighted.'

Elizabeth II, Queen of England, certainly looked content as she strode away to the hall, where dinner was awaiting her arrival.

Christine looked at Dancer. 'I hope you know what you're in for!'

Dancer whinnied and stamped. Mousie laughed. 'You haven't even met her, you bad boy! How do you know she's your type?' Dancer arrogantly turned his back on them and began to eat his hay.

Morgan called the stud farm from the telephone next to Dancer's stall, and made the arrangements. He then escorted Mousie and Christine in to dinner, and sat them down at a table of young riders.

Mousie liked them all, and was having the time of her life. She glowed with confidence as she was immediately made the centre of attention. Christine was gratified to see how happy her daughter was. The girls at school should see her now, she thought.

Christine made her decision. Leaving Mousie laughing gaily at a new friend's witty remark, she took Morgan aside.

'Morgan, I have to talk to you.'

'Certainly, madam, how can I be of service?'

Christine told him of Eddie's secret phone call that morning, repeating it word for word, and gave him a sketchy background of the events that had occurred in Canada concerning Dancer. The Queen's head groom was clearly upset.

'Madam, this is extremely serious. I'll handle it immediately. Thank you so much for your information. I'll get to the bottom of this, and see to it that you are not bothered further. My humblest apologies.' Morgan made a slight bow, and hurried off.

Christine returned to her seat, her absence unnoticed. She felt a great burden off her shoulders. She would let Morgan deal with Eddie. She needn't alarm Mousie on this momentous day in her life.

Dinner was delicious; clear soup first, wild rice, broiled pheasant, vegetables, wine, and for dessert, chocolate mousse and tiny, crispy cookies. After each course, servants appeared to clear things away, and bring on the next. Music played in the background. Christine thought it sounded like *The Phantom of the Opera*, but it was hard to be certain over the noise of people talking.

When the coffee was served, the Queen rose. There was immediate silence. Everyone rose to their feet.

'Thank you. Please be seated.' She paused while her guests sat. 'We're delighted that you all came to entertain us today. Some of you came a very long distance indeed. It was a marvellous show and we enjoyed ourselves tremendously. Now, to honour the winner of the competition, we wish to present this silver bowl. It is inscribed with the date, the place, and the name of the winner and the winning horse.' The audience gasped their approval. This would be a treasured item in any household.

'We would like Miss Hilary James to come forward please, to accept the bowl.'

Everyone rose as Mousie walked to the front of the hall. She was obviously a favourite among her peers, and modestly accepted congratulations from her new friends as she passed. Christine's eyes brimmed with tears of pride. This was a great day for Mousie.

The applause masked the sound of hooves. Dancer appeared at the stage just as Mousie stepped up to accept the bowl. He'd leapt out of his stall once again, pushed the swinging doors open with his nose, and trotted into the great hall. The crowd guffawed with hilarious disbelief.

'We neglected to mention that Daring Dancer should come forward as well. We regret our omission.' The Queen's eyes twinkled, and everyone laughed at her joke. She handed the silver bowl to Mousie, who held it up to Dancer for his consideration. He sniffed it with disdain, then looked away. He made a slight bow, then trotted out the same way he'd come. The room roared with applause and laughter. 'Such a showman!' muttered the Queen to Mousie and then laughed with the rest. Mousie nodded happily.

Mousie and her mother drove back to Clusters feeling mellow and ready for bed. The day had been exciting and rewarding, and they were looking forward to meeting Cassandra. The prospect of a foal the following year was a topic of conversation on the way back, as was the impending arrival of the Caseys.

'Why are they coming for just two days, Mom? Seems like a waste of money. I mean, we'll be home soon. Mr Casey could talk to you then.'

'Another one of life's little mysteries, Mousie.' She smiled to herself, warmed that Rory was so eager to tell her the news face to face.

'Should we call the airport, Mom? They might be trying to find us.'

'Relax. We wouldn't know which airport to call, let alone which airline. Anyway, they'll be flying tonight and we'll see them tomorrow. And don't worry, if they've come this far, they'll be sure to track us down. Your gran gave them directions.' Christine smiled at her anxious daughter and gave her a hug. 'Don't worry!'

They arrived at Clusters, and waved goodbye to Percy after making arrangements to be picked up at nine-fifty the following morning to see Cassandra.

Their beds called to them, and they gratefully tumbled into the down mattresses and slept soundly until the morning.

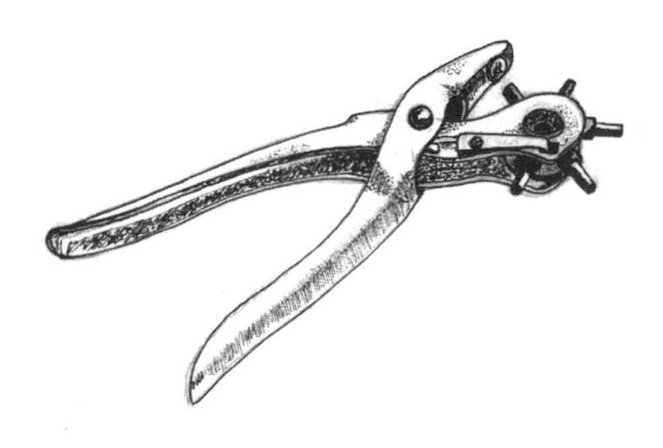

Chapter 9

The Hunt

CASSANDRA WAS BEAUTIFUL. Half thoroughbred with a Russian warmblood grandmother and a hackney grandfather, she was delicately proportioned, yet had substantial bone and a proud bearing. Her colour was a deep brown. She had a white star on her face and one tall white stocking on her back right leg. Standing sixteen and a half hands, she was healthy, glossy and definitely attractive to Dancer.

Morgan walked her out for Mousie and Christine to see, and Dancer got a good look, too. He snorted his approval, arching his neck in a distinctly stallionish way, and pawed the ground. She pranced for him, coyly, strutting her stuff, then whinnied loudly.

Morgan laughed and said, 'Love at first sight.'

Dancer was of unknown parentage, but he appeared to be thoroughbred with perhaps a bit of coach horse or Clydesdale in his history. He had good bone and beautiful conformation. Standing seventeen hands at the withers, he was a burnished chestnut colour with a dash of white on his elegant face. They would make an excellent match.

Morgan took away the flirtatious Cassandra to make preparations for the breeding. He had assured them again that the stable would handle everything.

He also privately took Christine aside and confirmed that he had dismissed Eddie. He was forbidden to go near Highgrove or Dancer, on threat of police action. There would also be a twenty-four-hour watch on Dancer until they left. She felt reassured, and couldn't think of any other precautions.

Mousie and Christine patted Dancer and made a fuss over him. Dancer pushed them out of his stall with his nose, impatient for them to be gone. They told him to behave himself, and started walking to the car.

'Is this how you'll feel when I get married, Mom? All nervous, and sort of happy and unhappy at the same time?'

Christine laughed and said, 'Well, this marriage is hardly for a lifetime.'

Caroline came running after them. 'Mrs James! Hilary! Oh, I'm so glad I've caught you.' She was out of breath. 'I've arranged for you to hunt tomorrow with the Beaufort. They're cubbing, actually. We hunt in the autumn, but cubbing is just as much fun. A few from this stable are going, so we can either put Dancer or Morgan's hunter on the horsebox for you.'

'Terrific!' Mousie couldn't believe her luck. 'Thank you so much! I'd like to take Dancer. I think he'll have a great time.'

'Whatever you think. Morgan told me that whichever you chose would be the right decision.' Caroline smiled as she caught her breath. 'Percy will pick you up at Clusters at seven-thirty tomorrow morning.'

'I'm so happy! I've always wanted to fox-hunt in England!'

'What should she wear?' Christine asked.

'Her show breeches are tan and her jacket is black, so her riding habit should be fine.' Caroline turned to Mousie. 'And wear your boots, gloves, and riding helmet, of course. I'll bring a stock tie and pin, and you'll be all set, Hilary.' Caroline smiled at Mousie. She'd grown fond of the leggy, spunky teen-ager, and was pleased to be able to give her a good time.

Mousie and Christine thanked Caroline, and headed to the car, which was parked just outside the courtyard. They walked past the great iron gate, turned the corner, and there, standing beside the grinning chauffeur, were Rory and Sandy.

Christine felt the blood rushing to her face as her heart lurched. She stared in disbelief.

'Christine!' yelled Rory, running to her and grabbing her in his arms. He gave her a big kiss, then pulled back to take a good look at her. He kissed her again.

'Rory!' Christine was delighted, and they both laughed aloud.

Sandy and Mousie rolled their eyes at each other as they watched their parents, then couldn't help but laugh, too.

'How did you find us?' asked Christine.

'Simple. Joy told us you were at Clusters. When we arrived, Percy here was outside with his car, and he asked us if we were the Caseys. We said yes, and he told us to hop in!'

'Percy, how did you know when they'd be arriving?' Christine asked.

'It was a little surprise we planned for you. Caroline and myself.' Percy blushed, totally pleased.

'You're really something, Percy!' Mousie marvelled, making him blush a brighter pink.

'Well,' said Christine, 'are you all checked in?'

'Yes, we're all set. Why don't Sandy and I treat you to lunch in Percy's favourite pub. It's at a little inn down the road. He recommends it highly.'

'It's the best for miles,' confirmed Percy.

'Sounds perfect.' Christine couldn't wipe the smile off her face.

Christine, Mousie, Sandy and Rory found themselves seated around an old oak table in the Bradgate Arms. The stone pub had been operating for over two hundred years. It needed freshening up, but its simple charm couldn't be denied. Every table was taken, and there were people standing with their ale, chatting to friends. They were mostly farmers and a few city folk who'd recently moved out to the country, or were merely passing through.

Their table was beside a window overlooking meandering stone walls that surrounded green fields inhabited by contented cows and sheep. Remnants of English stout, iced tea, and ploughman's lunch were on the table. They'd gotten caught up on the news over a leisurely meal.

'This is the life,' Sandy said dreamily, 'I've never been to England before. It doesn't look the same as it does in pictures.'

'Nothing ever does,' answered Rory. 'You have to experience things first-hand.' He pulled a snapshot of Christine and himself out of his wallet. It was over twenty-five years old, taken at their high school prom. 'You see, proof that reality is much better than pictures.'

Everyone burst out laughing, Christine most of all. 'I didn't know you still had that! Look at your sideburns!'

'Mom! His sideburns look better than your paisley headband! Did people actually wear those?'

'We were considered a very handsome couple, Mousie,' said Rory with a twinkle. 'And that brings me to the reason we're here.'

'Should Hilary and I leave?' Sandy asked his father.

'Only if you want some fresh air,' he answered.

'Let's go, Hil!' Sandy and Mousie raced outside, delighted to be free and away from anything serious. They'd been sitting too long, and also had no desire to stifle their parents' conversation.

'Could we have coffee, please?' Rory called to the waiter.

'Right away, sir.'

'Christine, I assume Joy told you about my divorce when she called to say we were coming?'

'Yes, she did.' Christine was careful. 'Congratulations. I'm glad Helena's ready to get on with her life.'

'Me, too. She's ready now to make it official, and that helps us all out.'

'How are your kids taking it?'

'They've known for years that things haven't been great. Sandy doesn't have any problems with it. He loves us both, and wants to see us both happy. I'm a little worried about Rosalyn, though. She's with her mother in Florida right now. She understands, but would like to see us stay together.'

'That's only natural, Rory. It'll take a lot of time for her to feel right about it. Don't forget, she's hardly turned eleven. Divorce is very hard on kids.'

The waiter arrived with coffee, and they waited while he poured.

'Christine, remember the day I came to your house upset and confused and asking for more than you could possibly give me?'

'I certainly do.' She smiled at him. 'How could I forget? I was miserable for months, thinking I'd probably never see you again.'

'So was I. I behaved like such a fool that day, I thought you'd dump me on the scrap heap where I belonged.'

Christine shook her head. 'I'd never think badly of you, Rory.'

Rory stared at his hands, unsure of how to proceed. 'And then, that day when I saw you on the road with Sam Owens. Remember what I asked you?'

'Of course.' Christine smiled warmly, eyes sparkling. 'You asked if I'd go out with you, once you got your divorce.'

Rory leaned forward, very serious. 'I'm here to ask that question again.'

The mood was broken as Mousie and Sandy came in flushed from the fresh air, and breathlessly asked if they could start walking back.

'Sure. Ask Percy which road to take, and we'll pick you up shortly, along the way.' Sandy and Mousie happily breezed out, full of youthful energy.

Rory continued. 'It'll take a little time for everything to be signed and sealed. We've pretty much decided on who gets what, so it shouldn't be long. But I have to know if you think of me the same way I think of you. I couldn't wait for you to come home from England. Even a few more days.' Rory looked intensely into her eyes, hoping for reassurance. He reached over the table and took her hands in his. 'I want to know if you'll marry me.'

'Wow.' Christine spoke quietly. 'Rory, let's not rush things. I want to spend a lot of time with you, and see how things go. I couldn't stand to mess things up because we were in too much of a hurry.'

'Did I do it again? Am I pushing too hard?' He was upset.

'Just a little. But don't stop. It feels nice to be courted.' Christine squeezed his hands and smiled impishly. Rory pulled her to him over the table, and kissed her right on the lips.

Sandy and Mousie walked along the country road, shoulder to shoulder. They felt that all was right in the world, having discussed their parents and England and school and friends and Dancer and how nice it was that they should be walking along a country road in England. Mousie was relaxed and enjoyed Sandy's company more than she had since the prom fiasco.

'Do you think our parents will actually get married?' asked Mousie.

'I sure hope so. My parents made each other miserable. Mom was out all the time, and until your mother started paying attention to him, I hadn't seen Dad smile in years, except for that night we liberated Dancer.'

Mousie laughed at the memory. 'You guys were great! That must have been scary.'

'No kidding! But talk about a rush!'

The day was getting a bit chillier and the sky was darkening, even though it was only about four o'clock.

'It looks like rain,' said Sandy, putting his collar up around his neck.

'Don't you think it's about time our parents picked us up?' Mousie shivered.

'We've been on this road the whole way, so they can't have missed us. They probably had more than one cup of coffee, they always do.'

A dark blue van passed them. Then a small red car. They kept walking.

'I want to tell you something, Hilary. Last week I told Sara I wouldn't go out with her. She had a fit. Called me names.'

'Really? What kind of names?'

Sandy laughed. 'Don't worry. Nothing I can't handle. But she said something that clicked.'

Mousie didn't know where this was going. 'What?'

'She accused you of stealing me.'

'What!'

'It's all right. But it explained why she's so horrible to you. She's jealous.'

'Sara? How could she be jealous of me? She's pretty and popular, and she's rich, and her uncle's ...'

'You underestimate yourself, Hilary. But that's part of your charm.'

'Sandy, you're making me very uncomfortable.'

'Why?'

'I don't know.'

Mousie wanted to tell him that she didn't trust her feelings about him. She'd thought he was going to ask her to the formal, but he took Sara instead. He'd seemed so interested in her, then confused her and caused her to doubt her reading of him. But she didn't dare say anything. She didn't know how he'd react. She decided to change the subject.

'We weren't supposed to turn anywhere, were we? We've been walking for ages.' Three more cars passed. And the blue van again, this time more slowly.

Mousie was starting to wonder. 'They can't have drunk that much coffee.'

'Percy told us to go straight along this road. They said they'd pick us up shortly. I guess "shortly" has many interpretations.' Sandy was starting to worry, too, but didn't let on.

'Anyway, I bet Sara's jealous that you win all the jumping competitions when her Uncle Sam owns the best stables in Canada. It probably frustrates her terribly.'

'Maybe. And she's not a very good sport. Do you think that's why Mr Owens wanted to buy Dancer? For Sara? Chad Smith said that.'

'Why wouldn't he? He'd want his niece to win, not you. But I guess Chad took it to extremes.'

'No kidding!'

'Is it all over, now that Chad's dead?'

Just as Mousie was about to answer, the blue van passed again, then slowed to a halt. A man rolled down the window and leaned out.

'It's Eddie, Dancer's groom. Hi, Eddie!' Mousie waved to him. Knowing nothing about his call to Owens, she was relieved to see a familiar face.

'Who'd you say that is, Hilary?' Sandy asked.

'He's a groom at Highgrove. Maybe he knows where my mom and your dad are.' They walked over to the van.

'I thought it was you,' said Eddie cheerfully. 'Do you and your friend need a lift somewhere?'

Sandy and Mousie looked at each other, considering whether they should take a lift to Clusters before the storm.

Just then, Percy pulled up beside them. Eddie tore off spraying gravel.

Christine jumped out just as their car came to a stop.

'You must've walked fast! Percy thought you couldn't have got as far as the fork, and we've been zigging and zagging all the possibilities! Are you okay?'

'We're fine! But we were wondering where you were.'

'Who was that in the van, Mousie? He sure took off fast.'

'That was Eddie, the groom. He offered to give us a lift.

We might've accepted, too, if you hadn't shown up.' Mousie was happy to see her mother. She didn't notice the look of shock on her face.

'Get in the car! It's starting to rain!' called Rory. They crowded in, just as the heavens opened.

Now Mousie noticed that her mother had something on her mind.

'Out with it, Mom.'

'All right. I was trying to decide on an appropriate time to discuss this, but I guess there's no time like the present.'

'Holy, this sounds like trouble!' Sandy said, joking.

'It is trouble.' And Christine proceeded to tell Rory and Sandy about the tussle between Dancer and Eddie. Then she told them all about Eddie's call to Canada, and her chat with Morgan.

'I didn't know that, Mom! We might've taken a ride with Eddie just now! And who knows what would've happened to us.'

'Honey, I should've told you. Morgan was handling things, and I assumed that only Dancer was in any danger, and I didn't want to upset you. But now I see that I was wrong.'

'How did Owens get his tentacles all the way over here?' Rory was angry.

'You can't assume it was Sam Owens, Rory, just because the call was to Canada. Eddie was in Canada with the Queen last fall,' Christine said. 'Who knows who he met there?'

'A weak person always shows his hand. It's possible he was put in a little black book for future use,' Rory muttered.

'And didn't Caroline say that Eddie had a gambling problem?' asked a bewildered Mousie.

'Yes, she did,' answered Christine. 'I'd forgotten.'

'Maybe his gambling debts became overwhelming and he saw this as easy money.' Sandy patted Mousie's hand in response to her sad look.

'My head is spinning,' she said. 'I felt so safe after Chad

died and Owens said he had nothing to do with it. Now I know it's not over.'

Rory was deep in thought. He spoke up, 'Well, Morgan should know about Eddie approaching you. I think the police should be notified.'

Christine agreed with him. 'We'll see him first thing tomorrow at the hunt. And I don't want to hear any more talk of Sam Owens. You all seem too ready to cast blame on an innocent man.'

The visibility was poor and the road home was treacherous. The rain was turning the dirt into slippery mud. The four travellers sat silent and troubled. When the lights of Clusters finally became visible through the trees, they all let out a sigh.

'We made it, sirs and mesdames.' Percy was relieved.

'Many thanks, Percy.' Rory spoke for them all. They ran into the inn, unable to avoid getting soaked.

A little later, after having hot baths and changing into dry clothes, the Caseys and the Jameses were sitting in deep chairs in front of a blazing fire. They'd made a pact not to open the subject of Samuel Owens, and they were feeling the warm snugness that's only fully appreciated when nasty weather rages outside.

The porter arrived to tell them that dinner would be served shortly if they wished, and could he get them drinks? He discreetly disappeared with the order.

'Coming to England was a great idea, Sandy.' Rory smiled at his son fondly.

'You make it sound like it was me running around the airport demanding the first flight out!' Sandy returned the smile with a wink.

'We're sure glad you came over,' said Christine, glowing with pleasure.

Mousie laughed. 'No kidding, Mom?' Then she asked,

'What are you going to do tomorrow while I'm hunting?'

'Hunting?' asked Sandy. 'Hunting what?'

'Foxes. It's an old English tradition,' Mousie replied.

'With guns?'

'No! With hounds!'

'Explain this to me,' demanded Sandy.

'Well, the hounds sniff out a fox and chase it, and we follow the hounds on horseback. The odds are against the hounds, because foxes are smart and hear all the racket, but if the hounds catch it, they'll make short work of it.'

'And this is a tradition?'

'Like in those prints and on placemats,' said Rory.

'It's so picturesque,' added Christine. 'The running horses, the hounds with their noses to the ground. It'll be beautiful to watch on a fall day.'

'It seems totally silly to me,' Sandy stated, good-naturedly provoking a response. 'All those snotty people wearing stupid costumes chasing a scrawny, harmless little fox.' He poked Mousie in the ribs as she bridled, and goaded her further. 'I always thought you loved animals, Hilary! Now I see the bloodthirsty side of you.'

'Bloodthirsty! Mom! Are you going to sit there and let him call me bloodthirsty?'

'You're on your own here, honey. Explain away. We're all listening.' Christine sat back, confident that Mousie could defend herself.

Mousie turned to Sandy. 'Let me tell you, Sandy Casey, it's done for a good reason. Foxes eat chickens, scare sheep, and spread disease, causing people to hunt them. Hundreds of years ago, the farmers got together on their horses with their hounds, to try to keep the fox population down. Foxes are a big problem in England, so most farmers welcome the hunters and let them ride over their land.'

'What about the anti's, then? You know, the animal-loving people who come out to save innocent little foxes. They don't think fox-hunting's so great.' Sandy was starting to get into the spirit of the argument.

'If you'd bother to notice, they're mostly all city people who don't bother to ask the country people what it's all about. They think it's better to throw gas bombs and set leg-hold traps. They do a lot of harm to the horses and hounds, not to mention people, and then have the nerve to say they're animal rights activists.' Mousie glared at Sandy. 'People should think things through before making judgements.'

'Well, that's a novel thought,' Sandy replied sarcastically. 'But maybe the activists think they have to get some attention to further their cause.'

'Maybe they do, but that doesn't justify their actions, if you ask me.'

'Someone has to stand up for the fox.'

'Someone has to stand up for the chicken! And the farmer! And the farmer's family, who'd starve to death if the foxes ate all the chickens!'

Christine and Rory laughed out loud, but the two teenagers continued their battle.

'Come on, Hil. You're not asking me to believe that you're fox-hunting on behalf of all the English farmers?'

'Yes, I am!'

'Holy! I've heard everything now! You don't think it'll be just a little bit fun?'

'Maybe a little. But those nasty vermin have no natural enemies, and they're over-populating. In Canada, the government calls it "culling" and people get paid to do it!'

'Only people who've studied the situation and know what they're doing.'

'It comes to the same thing.'

There was a slight pause, then Sandy said, 'Just admit that you'll have one heck of a fun time chasing around the country on Dancer, and we'll call it a truce.'

'A truce? You're giving in!'

'No, I'm just willing to make peace before dinner.'

'Peace in our time. I see politics in your future.' Mousie'd had her say and was triumphant that Sandy wanted to stop the debate. 'Okay. I'll admit it. It might be fun.'

'And that's why you're doing it.'

'I have to admit that, too?'

'Yes, or I'll start up again.' Sandy smiled.

'Okay, okay. That's why I'm doing it. But I'm not bloodthirsty!'

The drinks had arrived during the conversation, and now Rory took the floor. 'Raise your glass to Hilary's health, and for luck on the noble chase on the morrow.'

They all stood and clinked their glasses together.

'Thank you, thank you,' said Mousie with a mock bow. 'Now, back to my question. What are you going to do tomorrow while I hunt?'

'I'm following the hunt,' answered Christine. 'I've always wanted to see a hunt. And the truth be told, I want to make sure you're all right.'

'Me too,' said Sandy. 'Who knows? Even I, the protector of all foxes, might want to try hunting one day. I sure had a great ride the night we stole Dancer back from Sam Owens!'

'Shhh! Remember the pact!' Christine feigned mock anger. They all laughed.

'Then it's settled. We'll all go a-hunting with Mousie.' Rory raised his glass again, and they all went in to a sumptuous dinner.

Seven-thirty the next morning found them standing on the front porch of Clusters. It was cold, and yesterday's rain had subsided to a drizzle. Mousie was praying for the depressing weather to disappear and for the sun to shine. She was a bundle of nerves, not knowing what to expect of the hunt. She'd slept badly, too, plagued by an upsetting dream that she couldn't quite remember. It was also increasingly difficult for her to keep her distance from Sandy. He was good-natured and friendly, and she really liked to be with him. But she didn't want to get hurt again.

Christine was warmed by Rory's loving gaze, and Rory was feeling happier than he'd felt for years. Sandy was a little miffed that Mousie seemed to be ignoring him. She had him totally mixed up.

'Mousie, have you got everything you need?' Christine asked.

'You keep asking me that. Yes, I have everything. My hat, my gloves ... and what's this? Why do you keep putting Arabella's hunting whip in my bag? I've taken it out three times!'

'I haven't touched it, Mousie, and I'd thank you to lower your voice.'

'Well, do you think I'd take it out and put it back in myself?'

'Look, I don't know, but I do know that I haven't touched it all morning.'

'Do-do-do-do ... do-do-do-do,' sang Sandy *à la* 'Outer Limits'. Mousie glared at him.

Rory noticed the car first. 'Ladies, Sandy, our stage-coach arriveth. And not a moment too soon.'

Percy pulled up to the door, and got out to help usher everyone in. He looked around at the tense faces, and said, 'I'm so terribly sorry to be late. I fear I've caused you to become angry with me. The motor was dirty from the mud last night, so I took a moment to wash it. I regret that decision.'

'Percy! This has nothing at all to do with you!' Mousie was aghast. 'I'm all frantic with nerves, that's all. I've been a brat. I'm sorry, everybody.' She lowered her head in shame.

'Hilary, you're allowed. Get in the car, I'm getting wet.' Sandy humorously took her arm and helped her into the car. They started off, with Mousie in a much better frame of mind.

The skies started to clear as they neared the meet. Mousie was secretly convinced that it was a direct result of her prayers. Ahead of them were more than a dozen horse trailers lined up along the side of the road. People of all ages in riding apparel were unloading their horses, some animals co-operative and others stomping and snorting.

'There's Miss Caroline, just past the green truck,' Percy pointed out. 'Dancer will be in that silver horse-box.'

'Why don't I get out here, Percy? I can walk faster than you can drive through these horses.' Mousie was out the door and running towards Dancer. Christine could empathize with her tension.

As she neared the silver trailer, she called to Dancer quietly, and he whinnied his response. She opened the door at the front of the trailer, and cuddled his head. They were very glad to see each other.

Caroline came up behind them. 'Good morning, Miss Hilary. It's turning out to be a beautiful day.'

'It is, isn't it? This is so exciting, Caroline. I could hardly sleep last night. I've never been on a hunt in my life! And I had this strange dream.'

'Don't think about it, I'm sure everything will be fine. Let me tie your stock and you'll look like a seasoned hunter.'

While Caroline tied the long white cotton stock properly around Mousie's neck, Morgan unloaded Dancer, whose ears were pricked with interest. A young boy placed the saddle on his back and slipped on his bridle. In a matter of minutes, Mousie was up on Dancer, and ready for anything.

The small group of riders from the Highgrove stables rode amicably towards the designated meeting place on the Badminton lawns, where the master would give his instructions and the huntsman would gather the hounds. The sun shone through the mist, and Mousie listened to the sounds of horseshoes on gravel, hounds yapping, and people bellowing their hearty greetings. She thought she'd burst with happiness.

Morgan, Percy, Caroline, the Caseys and Christine stood at the fence, watching Mousie and Dancer as they entered the field. Christine noted that none of the other horses looked as fit. Mousie looked excited, and Christine was delighted for her.

She turned to Morgan. 'Eddie tried to pick up Hilary and Sandy on the road yesterday. It's worried me a lot.'

Morgan was shocked. 'He did? He shouldn't be anywhere near Hilary. He certainly isn't allowed near the stables. We'll have to keep closer tabs on him. In fact, we should consider calling in the law.'

'Thank you, Morgan. I'd appreciate it.' Christine suddenly noticed that Arabella's hunting whip was in her hand. How odd, she thought. She must've taken it out of the car with her. It felt warm.

Christine carried the whip through the horses to where Dancer was standing. 'Mousie, do you want to carry Arabella's hunting whip? I must've brought it with me.'

Mousie looked at her mother with confusion. 'Well, okay, since it's here. It brought me good luck at the horse show. Thanks.' Her face relaxed and she smiled warmly as her hand grabbed the whip.

'Have a great hunt, honey. And don't take any chances.'

'I won't. I don't know what I'm doing, so I'll just follow along.'

The huntsman blew his horn and the hounds gathered. Tails wagging and tongues lolling, they were impossible to count because they wouldn't stand still. The kindly, quiet gentleman resplendent in riding gear with cap and chin-strap leaned over to speak to her. He had ridden with Mousie from the trailers and had answered her many questions and informed her that there were 'fifteen couple'.

'That means thirty hounds. They're easier to count in pairs. We're cubbing today, as it's early spring, so we've got some puppies with us. Should be a good day after the rain.

The scent is better on wet ground.'

'Thanks for explaining so many things to me. You've been a real help. By the way, my name is Hilary.'

'Yes, I know. I'm Charles. You rode marvellously the other day. Won the bowl. Well done.'

Mousie took another look. She was astounded. 'Charles? You can't mean ... not THE Charles? ... What should I call you? Your Royal Highness?'

'Not while we're hunting, Hilary.' He smiled in amusement. 'Charles is just fine, or Wales, or Sir ... I answer to a lot of things, some more pleasant than others.' His smile widened with his joke. 'Mother told me to keep an eye on you, so you'll be seeing a lot of me, I'm afraid.'

'Oh, I don't mind at all. I mean, it's my pleasure. I mean, you don't have to, I'll be fine.' She was flustered, but the Prince was kind.

'I know you'll be fine, but I did promise. And it really is my pleasure.'

Mousie caught her mother's eye, back at the fence with the others, and made a small rolling eye motion for her to look at who was beside her. Christine stared.

'Caroline, is that the Prince of Wales?' Christine asked.

'Yes, madam, he does love to hunt when he can.'

In utter disbelief, Christine turned to look again, just as the horses were taking off. She could only see the back of his head, with his signature ears, riding behind her excited daughter.

It was a remarkable sight. From where they stood, they watched the hounds following the huntsman, then the master and the field master, followed by the field of horses and riders. They cantered over the rise and down the bank. They splashed through a little stream, and up the other side to the top of a knoll.

Please keep Mousie safe, Christine prayed silently.

The huntsman sent the hounds into the cover while the field stood. Half a minute went by. Then a solitary hound sounded. Another joined in. Soon, the whole pack of hounds was sounding in various pitches of howls and yelps and bayings, and then, noses to the ground and seeming to flow as a river of hounds, they followed the scent through the field. The huntsman took off in pursuit at full gallop, the master taking a different line with the field of horses. They were now out of sight.

'Shall we follow the hunt, sirs and madam?' Percy asked.

'Tally ho!' Sandy was exhilarated, literally jumping with excitement. 'Let's go!' They bundled into the car and followed the other cars that were driving along with the hunt. Rory squeezed Christine's hand. 'Never a dull moment with you lovely ladies.' They smiled deeply at each other.

They were going so fast, Mousie's eyes were watering. Just like in my dream, she thought. But she couldn't quite remember the dream. It left an unsettled feeling in her stomach.

They galloped around a little grove of trees, some of the horses struggling to retain their balance. Dancer was agile and light on his feet, so Mousie had little fear of his slipping. On they raced, rhythmically moving together. It occurred to Mousie that it was each to his own, that even though they travelled in a group, each person had to look out for himself.

The hounds were hot on the scent. They scrambled over a stone wall topped in brambly growth. They raced over uneven ground toward another, with denser brush. The field master looked for an opening in the scrub, knocking at it, trying to clear a place to jump. He backed his horse up two paces and sprang forward, scratching himself and his horse with thorns as they forced their way through. The riders found a haphazard order and each jumped in turn. Mousie felt the thorns on her knees and heard them claw at her breeches and boots. She smiled at the roughness of hunting compared to show jumping. This was fun.

Directly in front of them was a high, crumbling stone wall. They were near the front, and Mousie watched as horses scrambled over it, knocking loose stones off with their hooves. Dancer sailed over in a mighty leap, clearing it by half a foot and avoiding the fallen rocks on the other side. They roared through a grassy field of startled sheep and hurtled over the opposite wall.

Just as they landed, she heard a crash. She glanced behind, and saw a riderless horse jump the wall. She reached out with the hunting whip, caught its reins and stopped the horse. She quickly brought the horse away from the continuing rush of hooves, and called out. 'I've got the horse! Are you all right?'

Charles popped his head up and said, 'Yes, thank you. Quite all right. Oberon refused, then changed his mind.' He climbed the wall, his breeches a muddy sight.

Mousie held Oberon while Charles struggled up into the saddle.

'Tell your mother that I'll be looking after you!' she quipped. Charles grinned, and off they flew to catch up with the hunt.

The ground was boggy in a low area, and after thirty horses had travelled through, it had become a mire. Dancer bravely headed into it, followed by Oberon. Mud was up to their knees, and there was thorny scrub on either side, so they had no choice but to continue on. Ahead of them was a steep hill. The good news was that they were finished with the mud. The bad news was that the hill went straight up for ten feet.

Dancer made two valiant leaps and pulled himself up in a flash, Mousie holding tight to his mane and the martingale to save his mouth. Oberon, with considerable prodding from the Prince, did the same.

The horses had checked just ahead, taking a well-deserved

rest. Dancer and Oberon trotted along the deer trail, and joined the field. The hounds had lost the scent, and the huntsman was letting them drink from a reedy pond before sending them off again. Mousie looked at all the panting, sweaty horses, and realized how strenuous hunting was. But Dancer was having a great time. He enjoyed the challenge, and Mousie had never felt more alive. She smiled from ear to ear as she patted Dancer on the neck.

Over on the road, Christine watched through Percy's binoculars as her daughter trotted up to the group. She'd been very worried when Mousie hadn't come up the hill with the others, and now she let out her breath. She chided herself about her strong sense of foreboding. Everything seemed to be fine.

'Let me see, please, Mrs James. How's she doing?' Sandy took the glasses, and raised them to his eyes. He saw the hounds draw through the field, and take off, baying. The horses followed at a gallop. 'Gee, it looks like fun. Dad, do you think we could get Chunky in shape?'

'For you? Not a chance. Chunky's twenty if she's a day, and she's a hundred pounds overweight. Not to mention how your feet almost touch the ground when you ride her. Leave her in the pasture, Sandy.'

'But I really want to do this. I'll start riding lessons when we get back, and maybe by next fall ...'

'So, it doesn't look as silly as you thought last night?' Christine asked innocently.

'Not you, too? Will I never live this down? I was only kidding!' Rory and Christine laughed as they all got back into the car. Sandy happily pretended to sulk as Percy drove on to where the horses might be expected to appear next.

Eddie watched the scene from his vantage point behind a clump of bushes. He was dressed in dark hunting clothes, astride a powerful black horse. He pulled his riding cap low over his eyebrows and tightened his chin-strap. He adjusted his dark glasses. His instructions were clear.

On the fly, with the wind in her face, the sounds of galloping hooves in her ears, Mousie made a wish that she could capture this moment forever. She wanted to remember exactly how she was feeling, what she was smelling, what she heard, and what she saw. She squeezed her eyes shut for only a second, to make that wish.

When she opened her eyes, she noticed that the middle-aged woman riding beside her had lost a stirrup. It flapped against the horse's side, urging the horse to go faster, while the woman frantically felt for it with her foot. Mousie could see that she was quickly losing her nerve, and would likely fall off.

Mousie nudged Dancer over beside the horse. She called to the woman, 'Hello, there! I'll hold your stirrup steady.' Before the frightened woman could respond, Mousie reached out with Arabella's whip, hooked the stirrup with the crooked silver horse-leg, and held it firmly at her toe. The woman slipped her foot in, and smiled in gratitude. 'Thank you so much!' she called, as she gained control of her horse.

Mousie raced on, her thoughts drifting again to the dream she'd had the night before. It was about hunting, she knew that now. And Arabella was in it. What did she say? And something was reminding her of the dream. She shook her head. It eluded her.

The ditch in front of her returned her mind to the task at hand. She sat back in the saddle and loosened her reins to let Dancer have his full balance over the treacherous span. He treated it with respect, inching down the slippery bank as far as he could go and then thrusting his body across the deep water in a mighty leap. He cleared it safely.

Others were not so lucky. One man had a dunking in the muddy water and his horse ran off, but luckily it was caught by a friend. Another horse tripped over its feet in an effort to avoid the fallen man, causing the rider to flip into the ditch alongside him. The horses coming up behind veered left and right or scrambled through. Mousie sized up the traffic jam over her shoulder, concluded that no one needed assistance, and continued on. She wondered just how many more accidents to expect.

Reading her look, Charles rode up beside her and cheerfully said, 'We're a little soft, this being the first cubbing meet. Happens every year.'

'It's wild!' responded Mousie. 'Do people survive the whole season?'

He laughed. 'You most certainly would. And Dancer likes it, no doubt at all. You'll have to take up hunting to keep him happy.'

'He's good at everything he does.' Mousie was very pleased.

'I hope his progeny takes after him.'

'Will you send me a picture when it's born? I really want to know how it turns out.'

'Absolutely. This one will be special, I can feel it.'

'Already?'

'Why not? Cassandra is a first-rate mare and Dancer is rather amazing, you have to admit. Can't miss.' Oberon sped past them, Charles smiling broadly.

Mousie thought again about her dream, feeling ever closer to remembering, but not quite able to grasp it. They were coming up fast to a big stone wall.

Unexpectedly, panic seized Mousie's heart. There was no logical reason, as they'd jumped much higher walls in the show ring. But her teeth started to chatter and her palms were sweating. Her heart was pounding. The hunting whip went ice-cold. She could feel the sudden chill through her glove.

This very place was in her dream. This same wall, these

same crooked trees. It was happening now, just like in her dream.

Exactly like she'd dreamt the night before, an unknown man on a huge black horse came thundering up unexpectantly on their left side. He hurtled toward them at a sharp angle as they took off in tandem over the stones. In mid-air Dancer and the black horse collided, with horrific force. Dancer twisted wildly in the air, head flung back, eyes full of panic.

The rider of the black horse landed well out of harm's way, and looked back in satisfaction at the certain disaster. Mousie saw his smirk. She also saw the tree. He didn't turn forward in time to avoid the thick, low-hanging branch. It hit him head-on with a loud crack, knocking him violently off his horse and sending him flying into the mud and rocks.

Simultaneously Mousie, with her heart in her mouth, held on with her legs and gave Dancer his head. She prayed that he'd land on his feet. They spun in the air, Dancer's feet madly kicking, searching for a foot-hold. She could see the rocky, slippery ground coming nearer. Her head screamed in fear. Dancer landed awkwardly on his back legs, his feet sliding out from under him and causing him to skid backwards, out of control, taking desperate, backward steps. Mousie leaned forward as far as she could, well over his neck, to bring his weight forward and help him balance. By a supreme effort, Dancer and Mousie righted themselves, and it was all over.

The black horse raced on riderless, stirrups flapping and reins broken. The rider lay crumpled and still.

It was all in slow motion, Mousie thought, just like the dream.

The wind had suddenly stopped blowing. It was totally quiet, except for their raspy, panting breath. The hunting whip became warm again. Mousie's fear disappeared, replaced with limp exhaustion.

'What was that, Dancer?' Mousie whispered to her horse, stroking his neck with trembling fingers to calm him. 'What was that all about?' Dancer snorted, and tossed his head nervously.

Mousie's fingers tingled around Arabella's whip. Heat started creeping through her hand, and travelled up her arm. By the time it got to her neck, Mousie knew.

'Arabella,' Mousie said aloud. 'This was for you, wasn't it? You had to ride this ride again, and survive it, didn't you? Now, finally, I hope you'll be at peace. It scared the bejesus out of me, Arabella, but you deserve to sleep after your hundreds of years of unrest.' The heat calmed and soothed Mousie. She had no doubt that Arabella was with her, and happy at last.

Quickly Mousie cantered Dancer along the little path through the woods, full of amazement at what had occurred. She had to get help for the injured rider. She knew enough not to touch him. By the angle of his head, she was certain he needed professional help. And fast.

They followed the hoof marks of the other horses. Did Arabella's spirit travel in her hunting-whip? Mousie wondered. Had she been with her at the Queen's horse show at Highgrove? Is she still here, in the whip? They made a turn, and came face to face with Charles on Oberon.

'Hilary, there you are! Thank heavens! I looked around and you were missing, so I came back to find you. Are you all right?'

'I'm fine, but there's a man very badly injured further back. We collided.'

'Let's go!' The first person they saw was a whipper-in, a man who helps with the hounds. He radioed the hunt doctor, always on the ready when the Prince was hunting. Hilary told the whipper-in exactly where to find the fallen man, and then she helped catch the loose black horse.

Charles trotted up to Hilary. 'We're calling it a day, Hilary.

Oberon's had enough. Not as fit as Dancer. Would you like to stay on? I could arrange for Dancer's transport.'

'Thank you, but no. I think we've done what we were here to do, and we're ready to go.'

'How did you enjoy your first hunt?'

'I'll never forget it as long as I live!'

Nor could she forget it, as her head rested on the back of the airplane seat as they returned to Canada. She had many questions that needed answers. How had Arabella found her, and why? Why was Dancer threatened? Who was Eddie working for, and why? Why was life so complicated? She fell asleep, pondering these things.

'Hilary? Are you asleep?'

'What? Sandy? What are you doing here?' Mousie whispered, looking around at the darkened cabin and the sleeping bodies contorted into impossible positions.

'I couldn't sleep.'

'Oh. So you make sure I can't either.'

'You're not a morning person, are you?'

'If this was morning, I'd be a morning person. This is not morning.'

'You don't mind me being here, do you?' Sandy'd taken the seat beside her, vacated earlier by a woman who insisted on sitting over the wings.

'Be my guest.' Mousie struggled into a sitting position.

'I had a thought.'

'Congratulations.'

'Don't be sarcastic. I was thinking about what you said to me that night at Clusters. That people should know the facts before making judgements.'

'What I said is that people should think things through before making judgements.'

'Same thing.'

'Whatever.'

'You mean about fox-hunting?'

'And life in general. But this is my thought. You should take your own advice. About me.'

Mousie squirmed and stretched, then stared at him. 'Can you be more explicit?'

'Certainly. You seem to have judged me badly, based on one incident at the beginning of our friendship.'

'Go on.'

'Just because I took Sara to the formal.'

'Go on.'

'You should think it through.'

'How can I think it through, Sandy Casey, when I don't know what to think at all?'

'Do I have to spell this out?'

'Yes, you do.'

'Okay. The way I see it is this. You and I were getting along great until I came to pick you up for school that day.'

'With Sara Preston in the car.'

'Yes. And why not? Her place is on the way.'

'And she said you'd asked her to the formal.'

'Correction. She said we were going to the formal together. You jumped to a conclusion. Actually, that fact was news to me, too.'

'What fact? That you were going to the formal together?'

'Yes.'

'So why didn't you say that?'

'I was stunned. Then your face went white, and I didn't know what was going on, and then you said you weren't coming to school with us, and then it was too late.'

'For what? To tell her that you'd invite who you wanted to invite?'

'By the time I'd recovered enough to do that, we'd picked up Carol-Ann, and the whole school knew. And you avoided me and wouldn't speak to me anyway, so I really couldn't ask you to the dance. I called at least twice, maybe three times, but you never returned my calls. So I logically came to the conclusion that you didn't want anything to do with me.'

'Wow. I guess that was a reasonable conclusion. But I had no idea you could be so ... manipulated. I mean, if Sara made that up and you went along with it, well, what would stop her from doing it again?'

'You're right. And she keeps trying.'

'So what are you going to do about it?'

'About being manipulated?'

'Yes. And your weak character.'

'That hurts!'

'Well? If the shoe fits.'

'I do not have a weak character. I'm trying to make you understand the circumstances. I can't deal with women's games, that's all.'

'Remind me never to get involved with anyone like you. A grasping female could take you away with a little transparent stunt like that, and I wouldn't know what hit me.'

'It wouldn't be like that, Hilary! I promise. If you'll go out with me, I'll never let anything come between us. Sara isn't a fraction the person you are. And I never liked her anyway, I just never understood her. And now that I do, I can't stand her.'

Mousie was tongue-tied. Did Sandy just ask her to be his girlfriend?

'Sandy, did you just ask me ...'

'Yes. Will you go out with me? To the movies, to dinner, to dances, to parties, to just hang out?'

Mousie smiled. She put her hand very tentatively over Sandy's hand. Sandy smiled. He squeezed her hand tight.

Chapter 10

Hogscroft

SPRING TURNED into a sunny green summer, and summer gave way to fall. Fall was alive with vibrant colours, but it in turn made its exit, and winter arrived full-blown and brash. That February was one of the coldest on record in many years, and Mousie and Christine were cuddled by the crackling fire at Hogscroft on a Monday evening after dinner, in an effort to stay warm. Pepper contentedly burrowed into Mousie's lap.

Their trip to England the previous March had been wonderfully memorable. The Queen's silver bowl was prominently displayed on the mantel over the fireplace, and was now filled with snips of evergreens and pinecones, in keeping with the season. Its presence reminded them of those exciting days.

Hanging over the bowl, equally visible, was Arabella's silver-footed hunting whip. Mousie gazed at it now, thinking for the hundredth time about her beautiful spirit riding through the howling winds, looking for peace from her torment. Mousie still got a lump in her throat whenever she thought of her. They'd discovered the whip in their luggage when they unpacked. How it got there, neither knew. The staff at Clusters had known nothing about an antique hunting whip in any of the rooms, and insisted that they keep it. With their best wishes.

And Eddie the groom, she thought. She couldn't think of England without remembering that limp body. They'd told her afterwards. It'd been Eddie who'd deliberately bumped them at the stone wall. And died instantly of a broken neck. It was tragic, thought Mousie, and so unnecessary.

Mousie had been bothered by nightmares since that event. The brutal attempt on Dancer's life had shaken her badly. Images of Chad Smith lying dead on the floor of the barn and Eddie's twisted neck flashed into her mind, often when she least expected it.

Luckily they hadn't encountered anything nasty since England. Mack Jones had been informed of the near miss in England. He was watching Sam Owens' every move on the suspicion that he was the mastermind. It was impossible to prove anything, and Owens was being very well behaved indeed. His manner remained smooth and generous, and very indignant that anyone could think badly of him. Mousie shuddered at the very thought of him. He spooked her out, there was no question of that. He occupied a corner of her brain at all times, no matter how she tried to forget him. She just couldn't imagine who else could be responsible, no matter what doubts her mother held.

Her thoughts turned to Sandy. Her dark mood vanished. She smiled. What a great guy! Her smile widened to a glorious grin. They'd been dating steadily since their midnight chat on the plane, and had grown very close. They'd started grade thirteen together this year, and he was in many of her classes. Her old tormentors, Sara Preston and Carol-Ann, had been stunned and furious when she came back from England with the prize of the school dating her. This gave Mousie enormous satisfaction. She chuckled again as she thought of their reactions, and childish spite.

Sandy had been taking riding lessons all year, inspired by the vision of horses and hounds galloping full tilt over the fields of England. He rode with Mousie every weekend and they'd hunted together a few times in the fall. Spring cubbing would start in a couple of months, and he was trying to persuade his father that he needed a horse. In the meantime, he rented an appaloosa schooling horse and rode as often as he could. Chunky happily continued grazing in her field, and had attained a remarkable weight.

Christine lazily got up to put another log on the fire. She was deep in thought. She and Rory had been dating seriously for the many months since his divorce. Rory tried not to rush her into marriage, but he loved her deeply, and couldn't quite understand her reluctance. Christine, on the other hand, wanted to be sure that it would work out well for the children, and was taking her time. She loved Hogscroft and wanted to remain there, but Rory thought that since his house was bigger, they should live there, with rooms for all the children, and a guest suite for Joy. While there were still things to discuss, Christine very logically argued, they shouldn't leap in with both feet.

What wasn't logical, and what Christine wasn't ready to discuss with Rory, was the real reason why she was procrastinating. However much she loved him and no matter how much she wanted to marry him, her thoughts still turned to Peter, her departed husband. Her eyes filled up with tears at the thought. Peter. Her true love. They'd had so much together. Even during his long battle with that insidious cancer, her handsome, auburn-haired Peter had kept his marvellous sense of humour and refused to get depressed. He wanted to live every minute he had left. What he wanted above all was happiness for her and Mousie.

How can I marry another man? Is Peter in heaven, watching me? Would he want me to love Rory, or is it making him sad? Her mother, Joy, had told her that Peter would want her to go on with her life and find new love, but how could she know? Christine had to get past this irrational thinking before she could contemplate remarrying. This indecision and confusion was constantly on her mind, and was in danger of building a rift between herself and Rory. Rory had been patient. He'd told her he'd marry her whenever she was ready.

She settled back into her chair, watching the new flames greedily lick the big hunk of cedar. She wasn't quite sure how to work out her problem.

Mousie yawned and stretched. 'I need some exercise. I'm falling asleep in my chair!'

'Why don't you pick up the mail, honey, before you feed Dancer and the geese and Charlie. Neither of us bothered to get it today. Probably bills and junk mail. I'll start dinner. What do you feel like eating?'

'Something ordinary. We've been eating so well lately, my stomach is crying out for something simple.'

'That's what happens when men wine and dine us.' Christine chuckled as she pulled herself out of her comfy chair.

'Good thing the weekend's over!' Mousie stuck her wool hat on her head and grabbed her coat. 'See you in a few minutes, Mom.'

Christine, rubbing her back and stretching, went into the kitchen to check on their choices for dinner. She was looking through the fridge, when Mousie shot back into the house, hollering, 'Mom! Mom!'

Christine whacked her head on the roof of the fridge and slammed shut the fridge door. 'Mousie! What's wrong!'

'Mom! A letter with the royal seal!'

Christine slumped over in relief, rubbing her sore head. 'Don't you ever do that again! I thought something was horribly wrong.'

'Sorry, Mom, but this is exciting! We haven't had a letter from the royal family since last year!' She tore open the letter.

'We're not exactly pen pals, honey. What's it say?'

'"Dear Hilary".' She twinkled at her mother. 'Notice that it's addressed to me.' Mousie resumed reading.

'"We are very pleased to inform you that Cassandra has foaled. Early this morning, she dropped a perfect chestnut colt with exceptionally straight legs, a handsome head, and a sparkle in his eye.

'"Cassandra is proving to be a first-class mother, and dotes on him. We have every reason to entertain high expectations for this foal, as he is the exact replica of his father. We've named him Dancing Cassanova.

'"I have enclosed photographs of him, as you requested. Much enjoyed hunting with you. Oberon sends his best. Charles".'

Mousie pulled out the pictures and they studied them avidly.

'He's gorgeous, Mousie! He's wonderful!'

'He's anaemic, Mom! He's straggly!'

'Honey, he was just born the day these were taken. You can't expect him to be muscled and round. Give him time, he'll fill in.'

'Charles said he looked like Dancer. He looks like a daddy-long-legs! In an orange coat!'

'Honey, all newborn foals look straggly, I promise you. He'll be so handsome he'll take your breath away. Dancer would've looked just like that when he was born.'

'Well, I guess the Prince of Wales is happy with him. What else matters? If they're happy with a soggy rat with legs up to his eyeballs, then what's it to me?'

'Go feed the animals. And be sure to give Dancer the good news. He's a father!'

'I'll just tell him his son is healthy. I don't want to depress him by describing the little thing.' Mousie disappeared out the back door, convinced that Dancer's progeny was hardly a chip off the old block.

Christine hummed a tune while she whipped up a bacon-and-cheese omelette, delighted with the sweet little son of Dancer. She'd seen many foals in her life, and she knew that this one was exceptionally good. The Queen must be thrilled, she thought. And she loves her animals. Dancer's son will have a great home.

That night Christine slept deeply. Snow fell gently outside, covering the ground with a luxurious coat of soft white crystals. The full moon shone over Hogscroft, illuminating the cosy stable and the picturesque cottage nestled in the new-fallen snow. She was dreaming, eyelids gently fluttering.

In her dream, she was walking into her kitchen, intent on the sink, where dozens of potatoes lay waiting in water for her to peel. She picked up the worn, green-handled peeler in her right hand, and lifted a large potato out of the cold water in her left. The potato had gone to seed, and there were many long white roots starting to shoot out. She set the peeler down again and carefully began to break the eyes off the potato.

'Christine?'

She froze. She knew without looking that Peter had come up behind her.

'Peter.' She turned and saw Peter standing as she'd seen him hundreds of times before, his big eyes gentle and on his lips a quizzical smile. She stared for a long time, drinking him in. His favourite navy Blue Jays sweatshirt that he'd ripped chopping wood. The tattered green sweat pants that he refused to throw out even as they disintegrated in the wash. His unruly red hair falling into the cowlick that had caused him untold aggravation. The tall proud body that had been riddled with cancer at the end.

'Peter,' she repeated. 'It's really you.'

'Yes, Christine. My love.'

She flew to embrace him, choked with emotion, but she found her arms hugging only herself. She looked around for him. Peter stood beside her.

Christine spoke through the lump in her throat. 'Peter. There's so much I want to tell you.'

'I know, love, but don't say a thing. I have very little time; please, just listen. Christine, you've been worrying needlessly. I want you to be happy in your time on earth. You have a chance at happiness with Rory. Please take it. It's the right thing. I know you'd wish the same for me.'

His eyes held her with their intensity. Christine listened raptly.

'Christine, our Mousie will take the world by storm, whatever she chooses to do. And you, my love, must fill your life with things of this world, until the time when we meet again. For when we meet again, trust me, darling, there will be room for others. Earthly jealousies have no place except on earth.

'Now I have to go. My time is up.' He turned and started for the door.

'Peter! Don't go!'

He paused. 'I'll be watching over you and our precious daughter. I'll always love you.'

'Don't leave me again!'

'We'll be together again. I promise.' He smiled at her, and she felt drawn into his beautiful, familiar, loving eyes. Her panic subsided, replaced by contentment. She would be with him again.

Then he was gone. She stood alone. She stared at the doorway for a long moment, then turned back to the sink. She picked up the cleaned potato and began to peel.

When she awoke, she felt that something of great importance had occurred, but she didn't know what. As hard as she tried to drag it back, her dream remained elusive. And she retained a nagging suspicion that it had been something more than a dream.

Chapter 11

New Beginnings

MORNING DAWNED on a sparkling new world. Gone was the greyness and dullness of the previus day. The sun on the fresh snow dazzled the eyes and lifted the spirits. Dancer leapt all over the fields, kicking his hind legs straight up in the air and leaving his tracks in the virgin blanket of white. Charlie butted everything in sight, and the geese ran around in circles.

Mousie was eating her breakfast when she heard Christine's light steps dancing down the stairs. Christine laughed with joy as she observed the animals outside the window, and swept over to Mousie to give her a hug.

'Slept well, eh Mom? You're in a good mood.'

'I slept like a baby! And honey, I've decided to marry Rory.'

'Mom!' Mousie was amazed. 'What happened? Why so sudden?'

Christine paused to think. 'I don't quite know, Mousie. All I can tell you is that it's clear now what I should do. I should marry Rory.'

'It's about time. Let me call Sandy!' Mousie sprang out of her chair and pounced on the phone.

'Hold it right there! Keep it quiet at least till I get a chance to talk to Rory. He has a right to know first! There's so much to do, so much to plan. Oh, Mousie, I'm so happy!'

'No guff.' Mousie sat down to her cereal again, and took a big spoonful. She smiled at her mother as she chewed, marvelling at the overnight transformation.

As they went about their breakfast, they discussed the idea of combining families and how it would change their lives. Suddenly, they both stopped talking. They'd heard something. As they listened, they realized it was the clip-clopping of a horse on the road, getting louder as it neared. Christine and Mousie looked out the kitchen window.

Sandy was outside with a huge grin on his face. He was astride a tall handsome dark bay gelding. The horse looked to be a thoroughbred crossed with a Clydesdale, very strong and very safe. It had four white socks, the hind left reaching past his knee, and a white blaze on his face.

They grabbed their coats and dashed outside.

'Sandy! He's beautiful! Who owns him?' cried Mousie.

'I do! He's mine! Dad gave him to me this morning. Monsieur Lemieux, his friend from Montreal who fox-hunts, found him. Isn't he great? His name is Henri Huit, but I'll just call him Henry. He's seven and he's hunted three seasons and I can hardly wait for after school so we can go for a ride.'

'Why wait? Dancer!' Dancer appeared from behind the barn and trotted over to investigate. They were the same height, but Dancer was smaller boned and finer, even with all his muscle. They snorted and pawed a bit, but Mousie grabbed his halter before he could get into any mischief. Horses often fight before they establish their pecking order.

'Give me a second to tack him up, Sandy!' Mousie trotted Dancer to the barn, not heeding Christine who called out;

'What about school? You'll both be late!'

'We'll just have a short ride, Mrs James. I promise. And I'll drive Hilary to school. We won't be late.' Sandy gave Christine one of his irresistible smiles, and she gave up.

'Have fun. And be careful!' She watched the two handsome horses carry her daughter and Sandy over the fields at an easy canter. It would be difficult to feel anything but sheer bliss on a day like this.

Christine had just turned to go back into the house when

she heard the crunch of car tires on the drive. She looked around to see Rory leaping out of his car like a boy.

'Great horse, eh? I couldn't resist.'

'I should say not! He's perfect.' Christine gave Rory a big hug and a kiss.

'Whoa! I should drop by every morning!'

'Good idea.' They kissed again.

'Before we get carried away, Christine, I've got to talk to you about something.'

'Me too. Come on in and I'll get you some breakfast.'

Settled at the kitchen table with mugs of fresh coffee and toast and jam, Rory said, 'Helena wants the house. She wants me out, and she'd like to move in by summer.'

'Great.'

'Great?'

'Yes, great.

'You're happy that I'll have to find a new place to live?'

'No. I'm happy that you'll have to move in with us.'

'Christine, what are you saying?'

'That you and Sandy and Rosalyn are more than welcome to move in here.'

'I can't do that.'

'Why not?'

'Because we're not married. And you don't have to explain again why I shouldn't rush you. You know that I'd marry you tomorrow, heck, I'd marry you today, but I'm not going to mention it again.'

Christine paused, then said, 'Rory, will you marry me?'

He looked at her incredulously. His expression changed slowly from disbelief to belief then to sheer joy. 'You're not kidding.'

'No.'

Rory picked her up, swung her around and danced with her all over the kitchen. Then, overcome with love, he gave her a lingering, heartfelt kiss.

'I love you, Christine. I always have and I always will.'

'I love you, too, Rory.' And she meant it.

Sandy and Hilary raced across the snow-covered fields, laughing and free. Henry was fit and keeping up with Dancer, and the two horses were enjoying the run. They slowed to a trot as they started their return.

'This is terrific, Sandy! Why don't you leave Henry at our barn, and we can ride later?'

'Sure, if it's all right with your mom.'

'It'll be fine. There's lots of room.'

'Thanks, Hilary. Race you back.'

'Stop! These horses have to be walked out before we leave for school. If they're sweaty and hot, they'll catch cold or have muscle problems.'

'Oops. I have lots to learn, I guess.' He smiled happily at Mousie.

'We both do. There's always more to know.'

'Maybe you could teach me.' Sandy reached out across the horses and took her hand. Mousie stood up on her stirrups and leaned over to Sandy. She gave him a big kiss right on the lips.

Henry bolted to the side, startled by the sudden action, and dumped a dazed Sandy onto the snow.

'Sandy! Are you okay? Sandy, I'm sorry!' Mousie jumped off Dancer and rushed to his side. The two horses stood by, remarkably making no move to run home.

'Oh. Ooh. I think I've had it.' Sandy feebly moaned.

'Sandy, I'm so sorry I did that. I'm so stupid. I shouldn't have moved so fast. Oh, please don't be hurt.' She cradled his head in her lap and her tears fell onto his face.

'Fooled you!' He grabbed her tightly in his arms and covered her with kisses. Mousie shrieked and they struggled in play, rolling and laughing. Mousie leapt to her feet and made a dash for safety. Sandy persisted in the attack, chasing her and pulling her down. She made a small, playful gesture of resistance, then gave in to her desire to return his kisses. Completely enveloped in each other's arms, they passed a delicious few minutes, oblivious to the world and their horses' curious gaze.

Dancer stretched his neck over and gave Mousie a large nudge with his nose.

'School! Oh my gosh, I forgot! We'd better get back.' Mousie reluctantly untangled herself from the amorous Sandy's arms, and fetched Henry who was now pawing the ground in the search for grass.

'School? Who can think about school at a time like this?'

'Get off the wet snow, Sandy Casey, you'll catch cold.'

He rose to his knees in mock supplication. 'I'll willingly die of pneumonia if you'll give me one more kiss.'

Mousie grinned at him and jumped on Dancer, narrowly avoiding Sandy's outstretched arms. 'Let's get going, you lunatic.'

Sandy hopped onto Henry's back, and hand in hand they walked back to the barn. You wouldn't have been able to remove the smiles from their faces with a gallon of turpentine.

Rory and Christine were waiting at the house, ready to hustle their kids off to school. Mousie shot into the house to throw on her school clothes and get her books. Christine put the horses away while Rory and Sandy drove home for Sandy to change out of his wet clothes. Ten minutes later, a grinning Sandy appeared in his little red car to pick up Mousie, who was ready and waiting at the end of the lane. Christine figured that they would get to school mere seconds before the late bell rang.

Christine floated into the house. She knew to the bottom of her soul that she'd made the right decision to marry Rory. She had a lot to think about, and many plans to make. She called her mother.

'Hello?'

'Mom! I'm glad you're home. I've got some news.'

'Rory just called to thank me. He's giving me credit for changing your mind about marrying him. Of course I accepted. Always take credit when it's offered.'

'You're kidding! I've been scooped!'

'Congratulations, dear. It's wonderful. I'm so happy for you.'

'Thanks, Mom. I'm happy, too.'

'I can hear it in your voice. Tell me, what happened? Last we spoke about it, you told me that you weren't ready. You told me not to mention it again, as I recall.'

'I think it comes down to this. I was able to resolve my fears about betraying Peter. Don't tell me how silly I was, Mom. It was a real worry. But now, somehow I feel that Peter would be glad I'm in love again.'

'He would, dear. And don't think I ever thought you were silly. You had to work it out, and you did. It's important that you're completely ready.'

'Mom, you're great. Would you have some time to come help me get the wedding organized?'

'Just tell me when and I'll be there.'

'I'll talk it over with Rory and call you back.'

'Love you, honey. Bye.'

'Love you too, Mom. Bye.'

They set the date for the wedding. It would be on the twelfth of June, and they decided that they'd like a small wedding on the lawns of Hogscroft. With relatives and close friends, they estimated that they would have about fifty guests.

By May, Rory had the roof fixed along with the numerous other repair jobs that had long needed attention. The culvert was fixed, the shutters rehung and the house and barn and sheds were getting a fresh new coat of paint. Determined to sweep Christine off her feet, he declared an open budget on the Hogscroft refurbishing. He sent gardeners over to ensure that the grounds would be alive with riotous colour on the day of the wedding. He even had a new cream-trimmed hunter-green truck and horse trailer delivered as his wedding present to Christine. Rory wanted to make all of Christine's dreams come true.

Joy arranged the invitations, the catering and the wedding party's outfits. She bustled here and there in complete control of every detail. Conspiring with Christine, she ordered new green and white ivy-covered wallpaper for the kitchen and the painters were busy inside the house and out. The living-room furniture had been recovered with beautiful new fabric and the curtains were ready and on their way. Nothing was too much trouble. Each small decision deserved enormous attention, and Joy was revelling in every one. Workmen snapped to attention when Joy was in charge.

As the day neared, Mousie grumbled to her mother.

'Everything is changing around here. I can hardly study for my finals with all the redecorating and painting and gardening going on.'

'You're right. It's crazy in this house. What should we do?'

'Run away. But seriously, Mom, it's much worse for Sandy. His mother's after him to pack all his stuff and be ready to move out the day of the wedding. His sister Rosalyn is going to stay with her mother, and Sandy gets the feeling that his mother is making things difficult for him because he's moving in with his Dad. And really, it's not like Sandy'll be here much. He'll be away working for the summer and then he's off to university. She's not always reasonable. Or nice, Mom. She doesn't even talk to me, but so what. I don't see her much anyway. But it sure gets to Sandy. It's hard for him to study when everything around him is turbulent. For him and for me.'

'I see what you mean. And it's very important that you both get good marks. I don't have to tell you that. So, how can I help?'

'I don't know. Maybe you can't. Except maybe my room can wait until after my exams. I'm really happy we're doing it, don't get me wrong, but the last thing I need is to inhale paint fumes. Everything I'd learned would drop out of my head with the dead brain cells.'

'Done. I'll try to slow Gran down. It's not easy, you know.'

'I know, I know. She's like a ship, full steam ahead!'

'Mousie!' Christine laughed. 'But tell me the truth, isn't old Hogscroft looking good?'

'It's looking great, Mom, even though I loved it just the way it was.'

'So did I. Money won't make us any happier than we were before.'

'It makes a lot of people sad. They want more and more and more of it and it wrecks their lives. Some of my friends' parents are like that.'

'Do you think that'll happen to us, Mousie?' Christine asked.

'No. But I guess you get used to it real fast. Like, it's nice to be able to fix things up, and all that.'

'It sure is. Material things don't really matter, but it's nice to have them.'

'Yeah.' Mousie paused. 'I guess our money worries are over. I'm certainly glad I can go to university this fall without sending us into bankruptcy court.'

'That's if you keep your marks high. Now get back to work!'

Chapter 12

Owens' Revenge

IT WAS THE SATURDAY before the wedding. It had rained all morning, greening up the perfectly manicured lawns and flower beds. Mousie was slightly bored, her exams just finished and nothing to do. She sat with her chin in her hands looking out the kitchen window and observing that the rain had subsided into a grey drizzle. Pepper was asleep on her lap, twitching now and then as she dreamt of a squirrel or a cat or something else worthy of her attention. Diva was curled up beside her on the floor.

Joy and Christine were upstairs, putting the finishing touches on the master suite. It had been painted a creamy yellow, the old pine floors polished into a rich honey colour. Multi-coloured flowers intertwined with green ribbon graced the floor-length drapes and bedskirt and headboard. The king-sized fourposter bed was covered with an antique linen duvet and shams. The windowseats were cushioned, and embroidered throw pillows were scattered everywhere, giving the room an opulent richness. Oriental carpets harmonized with the velvety colours of the fabric, and Joy and Christine were hanging the watercolours and prints that would complete the room. The extra room next to it had been adjoined and converted into a luxurious master bathroom and walk-in closet.

Mousie's room, to her everlasting delight, had been completely redone in the image of their wonderful rooms at Clusters. Periwinkle-blue and white hunt scenes covered the wallpaper and fabric. Blue, white, green and red tapestry carpets lay on the hardwood floor, and there were dashes of red in the co-ordinating cushions. A beautiful white eyelet bedspread finished off the room to Mousie's satisfaction.

Tucked away under the eaves, a bedroom and bathroom had been created especially for Sandy. Since Sandy had said that green was his all-time favourite colour, the walls had been painted hunter green and the trim white. Matching green broadcloth curtains hung at the windows and a woolen green and white checked bedspread covered the spacious bed. White sheepskin rugs lay on the floor to keep his feet warm, and in the white three-piece bathroom thick green towels hung on the racks. Sandy loved it, even though he wasn't sure just when he'd be home long enough to settle in.

I feel like the fifth wheel around here, Mousie thought to herself. Mom is so engrossed in her decorating and wedding plans that I might as well be somewhere else. Don't I sound like the spoiled brat! Then, inspiration hit. Up she stood, knocking the startled Pepper off her knees right on top of Diva, who leapt up with wide eyes. She pulled on her riding boots and grabbed her helmet.

'I'm going for a ride! I'll be back soon, Mom, Gran!'

'Don't take Diva,' Joy called down the stairs, 'I have to take her shortly to be groomed.'

Leaving Diva looking puzzled and dejected, Mousie slammed the newly painted kitchen door behind her, and she and Pepper dashed through the drizzle to the barn.

'Hello, animals.' she called cheerfully. She was answered by a cacophony of sounds. The geese angrily demanded their dinner, no matter that it was hours before feeding time. Charlie jumped down from his window-sill perch and baa-ed. Dancer trotted out from his open stall, nickering, and Henry whinnied in his stall. Henry had been living at Hogscroft. It was a happy arrangement all around.

'We're going for a ride. I'll tack you up first, Dancer, then I'll do Henry. We're going to surprise Sandy.'

In no time, Mousie was riding down the road to Sandy's house ponying Henry along on a lead-line. Pepper brought up the rear, keeping Henry honest. If Henry tried to slow down, she'd jump at his tail, and hanging on with her teeth, swing a time or two until he'd kick out and speed up. He quickly learned to keep a steady pace. Mousie looked back at this sight and laughed out loud.

They trotted up the long paved lane to the Casey mansion. By chance, Helena was getting out of her silvery-blue Mercedes sports coupe as Mousie and the menagerie arrived. Dressed in an ankle-length black mink, fair hair swept off her exquisite little face with a diamond clip, Helena looked like a movie star. Mousie was struck by her beauty.

'Hello, Mrs Casey.'

'There'll be another Mrs Casey before long, won't there?' Mousie thought her words were slightly slurred. She noticed now that Helena wasn't too steady on her tall spike heels.

'Is Sandy home? I took a chance and rode over to go for a ride with him.'

'I can see that.' Helena pointed a long finger with a red-enamelled tip at Dancer. 'Is that the horrible horse that almost killed me?'

'Who? Dancer?'

'Yes, that's right, Dancer. He gave me quite a dance all right.'

'Oh. That's too bad.' She didn't know what to say. 'Do you mind calling for Sandy?' Mousie noticed that Helena was in no hurry to move from her spot.

'Well, you can't exactly ring the bell, can you? Not with two horses. You should've phoned before you came. Maybe he'll hear you if you yell. Or if you're lucky, he'll see you out his window. So nice chatting with you, dear.' She wobbled ever so slightly towards the house. Then she turned.

'What's your name? I keep forgetting. Someone has to make an impression on me before I can remember their name. Isn't that bad?' She smiled her lovely smile, perfect teeth gleaming in her perfect face.

Mousie remarked to herself how curious it was that this beautiful woman had ceased to be attractive since opening her mouth. Beauty is as beauty does, her mother had always told her. Here was proof.

'Cat got your tongue, dear? I asked you your name.'

'Mom. Why don't you come in.' Sandy, stern-faced, stood on the porch. 'It's raining. You'll get wet.'

'You're so right, my handsome son. What will I do without you?' Helena gave him a kiss on the cheek as she passed by and entered the house. Sandy looked at Mousie.

'I'm sorry, Hilary.'

'It has nothing to do with you, Sandy. Don't sweat it.' She gave him a dazzling smile and said, 'Come on, let's go for a ride.'

'I wish she'd be nice to you, Hilary. She was rude to you, and I'm sorry. It embarrasses me.'

'It doesn't embarrass me, so don't worry. Now come on, I can't hold Henry forever.'

Sandy's sad face broke into his adorable lopsided grin. 'One sec.'

He was out in less than a minute wearing his boots, hat, and rain jacket. Just as he was mounting, his little sister Rosalyn appeared at the door. She looked lonely and small and decidedly unhappy.

'Hi, Rosalyn!' called Mousie.

'Hi, Hilary.' Rosalyn looked at her brother. 'Sandy, she's been drinking again. I don't want to be here alone.'

'She'll just go to her room, Ros, she always does.'

'Yeah, but it feels, you know, cold in there.'

Sandy and Mousie looked at each other. They weren't sure what to do.

Mousie said to her, 'Why don't we tack up Chunky, and you can come riding with us?'

Her little face lit up like a Christmas tree. 'Can I? Really?'

Sandy laughed good-naturedly and said, 'Sure you can. Get your stuff, and we'll meet you at the barn.'

Rosalyn managed to gracefully spin around and leap in the air at the same time. She disappeared into the house as Sandy said, 'See that? That manoeuvre is what made Mom a famous dancer. It must be hereditary.'

'Your mother's very beautiful.' They walked the horses along the house toward the barn, Pepper at Dancer's heels.

'Yes. And when we were younger, she was really nice, too. I don't know what happened. Maybe the alcohol.'

'Maybe. I guess it ruins a lot of people. And it can't have been easy to be famous one day and a has-been the next. She had a serious knee injury, didn't she?'

'Yes. That ended her career. And started her on pain-killers. Which led to ... anyway, it's been really hard on her. I wish you'd known her before, Hilary. I think you two could've been friends.'

'It doesn't help that I'm Mom's daughter. I think she holds that against me.'

'Probably. She couldn't help but love you if she'd get to know you. But let's not talk about it now. Let's have some fun.'

They dismounted and led the horses into the Caseys' barn. Sandy opened a couple of stalls and put them in. Chunky was standing at the open end of the barn, where she could come in from the weather when she wanted. Mousie took her by her halter and opened the gate.

'She's a fat one, Sandy, we'll have to take it easy.'

'Rosalyn doesn't ride too much anyway. We'll go slow, then when she's had enough, we'll take off for a run.'

'Sounds good. What do you feed her anyway?' Mousie scanned her round palomino belly and fat neck as she brushed her off.

'She grazes on good grass all summer. Nothing to do but eat, I guess.' Sandy had come up quietly behind Mousie and suddenly wrapped his arms around her.

'Hey!' she squeaked in surprise.

'Don't say a word. I've got you covered.' He spun her around and kissed her full on the lips.

When Mousie could speak, she said, 'Hey. I like this.'

'I had to do that.' Sandy grinned. 'Hilary, I'm falling in love with you. Anyway, with Ros coming, I had to make sure we got at least one kiss today.'

Mousie laughed with delight.

'What are you laughing about?' a little voice asked.

'Rosalyn! I didn't see you come in!' Sandy started, dropping his arms.

'I just got here.'

Mousie caught Sandy's eye. 'Good timing.'

'What do you mean?' asked Rosalyn.

'I mean we're almost ready to go.' Mousie could hardly keep from laughing.

They tacked up and were outside minutes later. It soon became apparent to Mousie that however eager little Rosalyn was, she hadn't spent much time in the saddle. She flopped around on Chunky's back, flapping the reins loosely in the air.

'You know, Rosalyn, I could give you lessons after school anytime you want.'

'I don't need lessons. I'm a good rider. I want to jump in competitions.'

'Great. It's a lot of fun, but you'll need a little help. And Chunky needs conditioning.'

Chunky jogged along behind the others, catching up intermittently due to Pepper's not-so-subtle urgings. After only half an hour, she was huffing and puffing, her sides heaving.

'Let's go fast!' cried Rosalyn. She kicked her fat pony in the ribs, but she couldn't go any faster. Sandy chortled at the sight and leaned down to smack Chunky's bottom.

'Get a move on, fatso!' he yelled.

'The poor thing's had it,' said Mousie. 'Let's walk her back to the barn and cool her out. She's totally out of shape.'

'I'm not ready to go back yet. We just started!' Rosalyn was disappointed.

'It won't take long to get her in shape if you ride her a little every day. Sandy or I could get you started. But if you overdo it, she'll break down. You have to take it slow, Ros, especially since Chunky's an old lady.'

Rosalyn wasn't happy about it, but she realized that Mousie was right. By the time they'd walked back to the Casey's barn, Chunky was breathing normally and was mostly cooled out.

'You go ahead, guys. I can untack Chunky by myself.'

'Don't give her any water right now, Rosalyn, and be sure to brush her and pick out her feet. Can you do all that?' Mousie asked.

'Sure I can. I'll even put on her cooling blanket until she's dry and keep her in her stall.'

'Good girl!' said Mousie. 'You can let her out later, after you take off the blanket.' Mousie was gaining confidence in Rosalyn's ability to cope with Chunky alone. And Sandy would check on things when he got back.

'Bye, Rosalyn! Let's ride again soon!' called Mousie.

'Bye, Ros. I'll be back in a while.'

'Bye, Hilary! Bye Sandy! Thanks for the ride.' She waved to them as they cantered off across the field towards Hogscroft.

Sandy and Mousie let the horses speed into a gallop along the dirt lane beside the river. It was a perfect place for a run because the footing was good and there was no fear of ground-hog holes. Dancer was by far the faster, but Henry made a supreme effort, and they breezed along like the wind. After a while, the lane turned through some woods, past a large pond, and behind Samuel Owens' property. His huge mansion was barely visible from the path. They eased the horses back into a canter, and slowed to a trot.

Sandy was beaming, and called out, 'This is the best! Let me catch up!'

Mousie slowed down and they rode side by side.

'I've decided that I should stay with my mother after the wedding, Hilary. I can't leave Rosalyn. And I can't leave Mom. I won't be home much, but I think it's best.'

Mousie looked at him with surprise. 'I thought you couldn't wait to get out of there.'

'If it was only me, I'd be gone. But Mom's got big problems, and Ros needs me for moral support. I know Dad'll be there for her, but she'll feel better knowing I'll be home for Christmases and stuff.' He hoped she'd understand. 'I just don't feel right abandoning them.'

'Have you told your dad?'

'Not yet. I just made the decision today.'

'He'll be very proud of you, Sandy. I know I am.'

'You understand?'

'Totally. It'll probably be better all round. And it's not going to stop us from seeing each other on holidays.'

'Nothing could do that!'

Mousie turned to respond, when she let out a cry.

'Sandy! There's Chunky!' The little pony was behind them, running as fast as she could go, trying to catch up to the horses.

They cantered back and circled the wheezing pony, and Sandy leaned down and grabbed her reins. The right stirrup was gone, and the saddle was pulled halfway down her side on the right.

'Rosalyn fell off. Let's go.'

'Maybe Chunky broke loose,' Sandy said hopefully.

'Not by the look of the saddle. I just pray she's all right.'

Mousie led the way, Sandy following, pulling Chunky along behind him. They retraced their steps, Pepper going on ahead. She seemed to know what she was looking for, as she sniffed one side of the path then the other.

They lost sight of Pepper when she sniffed her way into the woods. She started barking short, high, urgent barks.

Mousie jumped off Dancer and tucked the reins under his stirrups so they wouldn't fall forward and trip him.

She ran into the grove where Pepper had headed and followed her barks to the other side of a big tree. Rosalyn was slumped on the ground. Mousie didn't dare touch her for fear of moving a broken bone. She knelt down beside her and pushed Pepper away from Rosalyn, patting her to show appreciation, but not wanting her to step on anything tender.

'Rosalyn? Rosalyn, are you okay?'

The little girl burst out sobbing. 'I followed you! It looked like so much fun. Chunky took a short cut through the woods and I hit a tree. Now I can't move my leg. Mom will kill me. My dance recital is this week.'

'Don't worry about a thing. Your mom will understand.'

'No, she won't! You don't know her!'

Mousie stood up, going over her options. They weren't far from Hogscroft, and Mousie's mom would know what to do. 'Stay here, Rosalyn. I'll be right back.'

'Sandy! She's in here!' Mousie ran over to Sandy and the horses. 'I think she's broken her leg. Take the horses to my place. Tell Mom what happened and get an ambulance. I'll stay with Rosalyn, she shouldn't move.'

'Right. I'll come back with the ambulance to show them the way. I won't be long.'

Sandy trotted off with Chunky dragging behind, led by her reins. Dancer pulled back and refused to go. Sandy urged and cajoled him, but he snorted and stood his ground.

'Go on ahead, Sandy. Dancer's fine here.' Mousie gave the horse a hug as Sandy and the two other horses headed for Hogscroft as fast as they could go. Mousie ran back into the grove, with Pepper and Dancer right behind her.

She took off her jacket and draped it over the pale, trembling little girl, seating herself beside her on the wet grass. To calm her, Mousie started singing a jazzy little song that her mother'd sung to her when she was a little girl.

'Once upon a time in a nursery rhyme there were three bears ... One was a mama bear and one was a papa bear and one was a wee bear ...'

After a short time Rosalyn fell asleep, her head cradled in Mousie's lap and her right hand buried in Pepper's fur.

The wind was coming up and the rain had left everything soggy. She'd forgotten lunch, and Mousie was feeling hungry. But it was comforting to have her little dog beside her and her big horse nearby grazing as the light was fading. Otherwise, she knew her imagination would be working overtime.

She wasn't exactly sure how Helena was going to take this. She'd probably think they should've helped Rosalyn untack Chunky. It never would've happened if they had. They hadn't even told Helena that Rosalyn was coming riding with them. The whole thing would look like their fault. And really, it was. Mousie didn't care what Helena thought about her, they weren't exactly close. She did care about Sandy. Helena was already testy with him about every little thing, and now the tension would get worse.

Mousie was lost in her thoughts, while Pepper slept soundly beside her. Rosalyn was dozing fitfully, jerking with pain every now and then.

Piercing the silence, Dancer suddenly whinnied loudly in alarm. Mousie snapped to attention. Pepper's head shot up and she jumped into the air, yipping once, then dashed through the brush. A horrible fight broke out. Growls and screams and barks and squeals and neighs and thrashing noises emanated from mere metres away. Mousie looked around frantically. She couldn't see what was happening. She had to get Rosalyn off her lap and run to help.

Mousie started to move her legs. Rosalyn awoke. 'What's up? Ow, my leg!'

'Don't move. The ambulance will be here soon. I hope.' Mousie was struggling to getting up to see what was going on. Her bottom was numb and one foot was asleep.

'Ow, it hurts when I move,' whined Rosalyn, in real pain.

'Be brave, Ros. I have to see what's going on.'

'But what if I'm left alone and you get hurt?' The little girl grabbed Mousie's legs and began to sob. The pain and fear mixed together was too much for her to bear.

Pepper continued to bark, her pitch rising in intensity. Dancer was putting up a real fight, and Mousie thought she heard a man cursing.

'Sweetheart,' Mousie impatiently cooed to Rosalyn. 'Let go of me. Everything will be fine. I'll be back in a minute.'

She finally untangled herself from Rosalyn and jumped to her feet. She listened. She heard people coming. Sandy and two paramedics carried a stretcher into the grove and put it down beside them.

'Sandy! Thank God!' Her relief upon seeing his friendly face caused her knees to buckle slightly.

'What's that noise?' Sandy asked.

'It's Dancer. And Pepper. They're fighting something. Please help!'

Sandy raised his eyebrows in alarm and shouldered through the thicket. 'Stay with Ros, Mousie! Joe, Paul, come with me.'

The two paramedics ran in after him. Mouse knelt down to quiet the frightened little girl, and they listened, transfixed, to the brutal sounds of men fighting. Then all the noises stopped.

'Sandy? What is it?' Mousie called out, tense.

'Joe, get some rope! Quick!' Sandy's voice was urgent and out of breath.

One of the paramedics appeared. He pulled a length of

bandage and a rope out of his kit and dashed back into the thicket. Deep voices rumbled and argued in the trees. Mousie and Rosalyn listened intently, but couldn't understand what was being said.

Pepper emerged first, filthy and bloody. She flopped on the ground at Mousie's side.

Sandy appeared next, looking grim. His arm was firmly grasping a lunging Samuel Owens, who was bound and gagged with bandage.

Mousie gasped aloud, 'Sam Owens! Oh, my God!'

Horror-stricken, she gaped at him. Owens' leg was ripped open, and he was limping badly. One paramedic was holding Owens' other side and the other walked behind him, holding the rope. All the men were muddy and scratched, their clothes torn. Owens looked wild, as though he'd gone over the edge of sanity. He struggled and made grunting noises through the gag.

Mousie's heart pounded in her ears. A sickening fear grew in her belly.

'Dancer,' she sputtered, springing into action, 'Dancer!' Mousie started into the thicket.

Sandy stopped her, his eyes worried. 'Hil, you won't like what you see.'

Ignoring Sandy's entreaties and shaking off the fear that electrified her body, she pushed blindly through the bushes.

She stopped dead. Dancer was down on the ground. His silky chestnut coat was darkened with sweat, and blood was oozing out of a gash on his neck. His sides were heaving from exertion, his mouth foaming, eyes bugged. His front left leg was bound up in the reins.

She dropped to his side, swallowing the bile that rose in her throat. 'Dancer!'

The big horse nickered at her voice, blood gurgling in his

throat. He nudged her with his nose and cuddled into her embrace.

Mousie held him, silent tears running down her face. 'Please don't die, Dancer. I love you,' she whispered.

Dancer tried to lift his head to tell her that he'd be all right, that it wasn't her fault, that he loved her, too. His head thumped down. His breathing was difficult.

'Sandy!' she yelled. 'Sandy! Get the vet! He's dying!'

Sandy came on the fly, answering her call. He knelt beside her and put his comforting arm around her shoulder.

'I've radioed ahead. Your mother is on her way with the trailer. Dr Masters is out this way and he'll be here soon. Are you hearing me, Hilary?'

Mousie nodded, her eyes staring blankly at Dancer.

'Sam Owens is tied up in the front seat and they're putting Ros in the ambulance now. The police are meeting us at emergency in Brampton to arrest Owens.'

Mousie nodded again. She peeled her gaze away from Dancer and looked squarely at Sandy. 'You go. I'm fine. Really. And Sandy, thanks.' She squeezed his hand tightly and kissed it, leaving a salty smudge from her tears. She turned back to her beautiful, dying animal.

Sandy stood. He wanted to stay. He longed to hold her in his arms and wait with her, to share her grief. But there was no choice. He turned and went.

Mousie hugged Dancer's head, tears of frustration and anger and helplessness rolling down her face.

She felt a warm tongue licking her ankle. She looked behind to see little Pepper. Confused and distressed, Pepper wanted to make everything fine again. Mousie hugged the little dog to her chest.

Mousie knew that Dancer's chances of living were slim, even with an iron will as strong as his. He'd lost a lot of blood, and was making no effort to stand. That was a very bad sign. A horse fights to be on his feet. She went to work immediately, and very gently untangled and released him from the reins and leather that bound him. She soothed and stroked him, praying in her heart that he would live.

And she remembered. She imagined him at the Royal Winter Fair, effortlessly springing over the highest hurdle. She thought of him taking a bow to the Queen. She remembered how he'd kicked Chad Smith and saved her life. And how he valiantly averted death at the stone wall in England. She felt a bond with this animal that could never be broken. There would never be another horse like Dancer.

Then, out of the corner of her eye, she noticed a glint of steel. A large jagged hunting knife with a leather hilt and brass plate was lying just inches from Dancer's hind leg. Careful to retain the fingerprints, she picked it up with her sleeve. It was inscribed 'Samuel Owens, Canadian Huntsman Award, 1981'.

'Exhibit A,' murmured Mousie. A knife like that could've done the ultimate damage, she thought. She felt angry. What kind of depraved and revolting human maliciously injures an innocent animal? He'd tried to kill Dancer. And perhaps he'd succeeded.

Christine pulled up with the truck and horse-trailer. She jumped down and ran to Mousie, taking her in her arms.

'Honey, everything's going to be all right.' She brushed away Mousie's tears and kissed her on the cheek. She looked long and hard at her daughter, gauging the damage. To her relief, she saw that Mousie was still strong. Now, Christine turned her attention to Dancer. 'He's bad, isn't he, honey.'

Mousie nodded. 'Real bad. Do you think he'll live, Mom?'

Christine secretly thought he'd die for sure. His breathing was laboured and shallow, his coat stiffening as he lay still. But she said, 'Dr Masters is minutes away, Mousie. He's the best there is. He'll do everything he can.'

Mousie wasn't fooled by the words, but she wasn't ready to give up hope. She resumed her position on the ground beside him.

Christine had brought blankets. She dragged them out of the truck and draped them gently over him in an effort to retain body heat. Mousie tucked them in around his sides. Dancer snorted weakly.

The sound of tires on gravel alerted them to the arrival of the vet. Christine ran out to the lane and flagged him down. 'It's him, Mousie! Alan, over here!'

Alan Masters wasted no time. He left his student assistant to bring the emergency equipment from the truck, and he dashed to Dancer's side.

If he was alarmed by the sight, he gave no sign. He immediately went to work. He checked Dancer's eyes, tested the texture and colour of his gums, took his pulse. The vet's mouth was pursed in a serious frown, but Christine and Mousie had no idea what he was thinking, and didn't feel they should interrupt him to ask. He assessed the neck wound, and tested Dancer's reflexes.

The assistant arrived with the emergency kit and Alan Masters gave Dancer shots of antibiotic and anti-shock, and started pumping plasma into him intravenously. He bathed and disinfected the gash on Dancer's neck. Deftly he shaved the skin around it with battery-powered shears and skilfully sewed it together with a long curved needle, using twelve stitches for each layer. He worked with precision and speed.

'Will he live, Alan?' Christine asked quietly, when he was done.

'That's yet to be seen. He's lost a lot of blood, and it's hard to say what other damage has been done.'

'Should he be moved? The ground is wet.'

'Let's give the drugs a minute before we think of moving him. We'll have to do it soon, though. If he stays on his side much longer, his organs will . . .'

As the vet spoke, Dancer made a rumbling noise from the bottom of his chest.

'What's that mean?' asked a terrified Mousie.

'I don't know wh ...' Dr Masters started saying, when the noise sounded again even louder.

Dancer began to shake. His legs shot out straight and violently twitched. His head thrust forward suddenly, then he relaxed. He exhaled a long raspy sigh.

'Get back!' ordered Dr Masters. 'Stay out of his way.'

'Dancer!' moaned Mousie. 'Don't die!' Christine held her daughter tight, comforting as well as restraining her.

With a monumental effort, Dancer pushed and grunted, then lay quiet again for a few seconds. He lifted his head, muscles straining, then rested it on the ground. In the next instant, with great determination, he tucked his back legs under him, positioned his front legs, threw up his head, and victoriously shoved himself onto his feet. He shook his head and tried to clear his brain. He took a shaky step, and almost fell over. He steadied himself, and then braced his legs in a splayed position.

Alan Masters was incredulous as he stepped forward. 'Well, I've never seen anything quite like it!' He checked Dancer's heart and lungs and legs. He looked into his eyes and rechecked his gums. 'Well, well, well.'

'Well, what?' asked Mousie.

'Well, it's too soon to say, but he'll very likely survive.'

Mousie and her mother were so shocked by the whole experience that they stood planted where they were. Then the reality hit them and they ran to Dancer. Relieved and exhausted, they fussed over him thankfully. Dancer nickered his appreciation, but was very weak.

Mousie and Christine blanketed him. Then Dr Masters gave him another shot and helped them carefully load the injured animal onto the trailer. He was stiff and wobbly, his head held low, and he seemed to be in danger of falling over.

But they finally got him on and lifted the ramp shut.

'I'll follow you to Hogscroft and check him again,' Alan Masters said. 'I'll honk if he's falling or weaving. I'll want to keep a very close eye on him for the next few days.'

'Thanks, Alan,' said Christine. 'You saved his life.'

Christine drove very slowly over the bumps and holes in the lane. She was aware of how concerned Mousie was for their passenger.

'Mousie, how are you feeling? Are you okay?'

'Yes, I guess so, Mom. I feel so, I don't know, exhausted. And lucky! I know Dancer's going to be fine, I can feel it. I mean, to get up on his feet like that. I think he made his decision to live, Mom, when it would've been easier to close his eyes and die.' Mousie wiped a tear from her eye. She was shaking a little. 'But I'm mad, too! What kind of person goes after a horse with a knife?'

'A very sick one. Pepper knew what kind of person Owens was from the beginning. And your grandmother tried her best to warn me. But Owens was caught in the act. There's nobody else he can blame. There's no suspicion he can cast, nor accusation he can defer. In other words, he can't squirm out of it this time. He's out of our lives, Mousie. At last.'

Mousie smiled. It felt good to smile.

Chapter 13

Dénouement

MOUSIE WAS CAREFUL to drape a blanket over the old swing. It was a giant inner tube that her father had hung with a rope in the old maple tree, many years ago. Somehow it seemed to her that it was entirely appropriate that she should spend some quiet time here, on this day, the day of her mother's wedding.

She was dressed in an ankle-length, lacy, apricot cotton gown. It had a scooped neck and cap sleeves, streamlined into a flaring skirt. Mint-green buttons fastened the front. Flowers were woven into mint-green ribbon forming a wreath around her head; the ribbons flowing down into her long silky hair at the back. Flat satin shoes had been dyed the same shade of apricot as her dress, and Gran had even found apricot panty-hose. She'd decided to wear the gold locket that her dad had given her on her eleventh birthday.

Dancer was almost one hundred percent recovered. Thankfully the stitched-up wounds were healing well and his muscles were rested and strong. Alan Masters still couldn't believe he'd pulled through. He said to anyone who'd listen that no other horse would've survived the attack.

Mousie's thoughts turned to Samuel Owens as she swung. The trial was set for September. Most likely after a very messy and public trial, he would serve his time in a mental institution. His high-priced Toronto lawyers had insisted on a psychiatric evaluation after Owens had called them from the police station. The whole story had come out, much to the horror and morbid entertainment of the gossips in the community. The last few days had been like a soap opera, with snippets of stories told at the post office in Cheltenham, the general store in Inglewood, and the tack shops in Erin. Owens had tried everything he could think of to own Dancer, consequence be damned, and when he couldn't take him alive, he wanted him dead. He'd almost succeeded.

He told the police that he'd seen Dancer grazing unattended from his den window. He could see the lane using binoculars. Dancer stood in sight, unguarded, at the thicket, while Mousie was busy tending to Rosalyn. He'd grabbed his prized hunting knife from where it was mounted on his wall, and stealthily crept up on Dancer downwind, not to be detected. Dancer was at a great disadvantage, wearing his tack. Once Sam had him by the reins, all the horse could do was kick and heave and thrash. He'd managed to crack four of Sam's ribs and damage his left knee. Pepper had by then entered the fight and wouldn't give up. She'd never lost a battle and had no intention of losing this most important one. She also won a chunk of Owens' leg.

He was a man obsessed, thought Mousie, and he had tried to do an unspeakable thing. Her stomach clenched at the thought.

Not only was he accused of all the Dancer-related incidents, including paying Chad and Eddie to try to kill the horse, but several other sabotage cases involving his out-of-favour employees and his competition. The trial of Samuel Owens would be of great interest for miles around. Personally, she hoped he'd be sentenced to solitary confinement for the rest of his despicable life, and Mousie would never have to worry about him again.

Mousie noticed Rosalyn over by the patio. She was feeling better. Her leg had been set and put in a giant cast, from hip to toe. She was cheerfully hobbling around on crutches in a dress identical to Mousie's, insisting that people autograph her cast. Mousie admired her spunk. Helena was furious that

Ros couldn't perform at her dance recital, so Sandy had been grounded from going to the wedding. She was being hysterical and unreasonable, putting Sandy in an awkward position. Unless she had a drastic change of heart in the next hour, or Sandy decided to come anyway, Rosalyn would be the only Casey child to witness the event.

Mousie was very happy for her mother. It was a perfect match. She couldn't ask for a kinder, more wonderful stepfather. And since she was going off to school in the fall, she felt better about leaving her mother now that there was someone else in her life.

All these things Mousie thought about.

And her father. She missed him terribly, especially now at her mother's wedding. Why did he have to die? She didn't feel like talking to any of the wedding guests at the moment. She was wearing her father's locket, sitting alone in her father's swing.

She opened the locket delicately. Her dad's strong, kind face looked out at her. Mousie's eyes brimmed over. My mascara will run, she thought. I better get a grip. But it only got worse. Tears streamed down her face, and she sobbed quietly.

'Daddy, I miss you,' she whispered under her breath, 'I'll always miss you. No one can ever take your place.'

Mousie let herself drift, remembering all the good times they'd had together. Their camping trips, weeks at rented cottages, shows they'd enjoyed together, times she'd needed his strength and times she'd cheered him up. As she swung gently back and forth, her head resting on the back of the inner-tube, she felt lulled and comforted until she fell into a dreamy, peaceful state. It seemed that she was floating on a big, billowing cloud in a vast sky of purest blue. Her father's face came into view.

'Mousie. My little Mousie, I'm here.'

'Dad?' She found that she didn't want to move. She wanted to remain floating, talking to her beloved dad.

'Just for a minute, honey, I can't stay long.'

'I'm glad you're here, Dad, I was just thinking about you.'

'I know, honey. That's why I came. Don't be sad, Mousie, be happy. I want you to remember me, it's true, but I don't want to make you cry. Don't worry about me.'

'I guess I was worrying more about me. I miss you, Dad, and so does Mom.'

'I know that, Mousie. It can't be helped. All you can do is go on with life, and live it to the fullest. Do what fulfils you and makes you happy with yourself. It all ends too soon. That's why I'm glad that your mother is marrying Rory. He's a terrific man, and believe me, up here we know.

'And your friend Sandy is a fine young man. Just don't let your hormones carry you away too soon.'

'A lecture from the grave, Dad?'

He laughed his old, booming, familiar laugh. 'My Mousie. Never change.'

'I love you, Dad.' His image misted over with her tears.

'I love you, too. For eternity. I'll always be your greatest admirer, Mousie. You may not know it, but I've been watching over you.'

'Somehow I think I knew that. Since you're here, Dad, can I ask you a question?'

'Shoot.'

'This sounds a little crazy, I know, but you said you've been watching over me, right?'

'Right.'

'Well, sometimes I get the feeling, and this is the crazy part, that you're looking at me through Dancer's eyes.'

'Oh? Really?'

'Yes. I sometimes think that Dancer is, well, you.'

'Is this a compliment?'

'I'm trying to be serious, Dad!'

'Sorry.' He chuckled, then asked, 'You were saying?'

'It's mostly when I'm in trouble. Like when Chad Smith

was going to kill me, or when Dancer and I almost flipped in England at the wall. He seems to look after me, you know? He seems to know just what to do. Like you, Dad. And when Sara Preston and the girls made my life miserable, it was only really Dancer I'd want to talk to, well, and Mom, but she'd be upset, where Dancer just seemed to be thinking the things you'd be telling me if you were still alive, and I'd feel better. But especially when I'm lonely for you, Dad. I somehow feel you're there. You know?'

'I'm glad, Mousie, that your memory of me is so strong. The comfort I long to give you, is coming to you through Dancer.'

'So it's true? You go into his body, and you're actually right beside me? Like a guardian angel?'

'Not quite, honey. But it comes to the same thing, doesn't it? You know me well enough to predict what I would say or do, and you feel that Dancer is transmitting that. And the happy result is that I remain alive to you.'

'Maybe that's true. I sure think of you often.'

'And the best part is that you only remember the good things. You forget my human failings.'

'Like what happened to the environment when you ate beans?'

'Now just a minute ...' He rose to their old jokes.

'And how the house used to rattle with your snores?'

'Hold on, Mousie, I didn't mean that you should ...'

'Or how you'd eat all the leftovers, and, ahem, EVEN the pie?'

'Okay! So you haven't forgotten my human failings!' His laughter boomed again.

'And I loved every one of them. Maybe not at the time, but I miss them now.'

'And I miss you. And your mother. But I don't feel that I've lost you, nor you me. We're bound by the mysteries of the patterns of life.'

'Wow, that sounds profound.'

'Do you understand?'

'I think so, Dad. I'll have to ruminate on that.'

'It's time for me to go, Mousie. I'll be watching over you.'

'Thanks, Dad. For watching over me, and for talking to me.'

'You may not remember …'

And he was gone. Faded into the blue, blue sky. The fluffy cloud got harder, and when Mousie moved her arm, it scraped against the tree. She awoke sharply. 'Ouch!'

Her face felt wet. It was covered in tears.

Mousie patted her eyes with cold water and fixed her makeup. From the upstairs bathroom window she could see that the wedding was almost ready to begin. She must hurry or she'd hold things up and incur the wrath of Joy, who'd planned things down to the millisecond. She galloped down the stairs and ran smack into Sandy.

'Whoa, girl! Where've you been? I've been looking for you everywhere.'

She hugged him tightly, then looked at him as she remembered. 'Why are you here? Did your mother change her mind?'

'Sort of. She's totally out of it. I asked her if I could come, and she mumbled something that I chose to interpret as a yes.'

'Naughty boy! I'm so glad.' They wrapped their arms around each other in an emotional embrace.

'Let's go.' Sandy took her by the hand and led her outside into the brilliant June sunshine. It was a perfect day. The air was mellow and a gentle breeze carried the aroma of a thousand flowers. The guests were already seated in rows of chairs that formed the outdoor shrine. The altar was created with a bower of twining roses, lily of the valley, peonies, freesia, daffodils, forget-me-nots, blue-bells and tulips. Huge bouquets graced the aisle. It was a beautiful sight.

Rory and Christine had decided that the wedding would be very simple. There would be only two bridesmaids, Mousie and Rosalyn, who was making a meal out of her incapacity to walk elegantly up the aisle on crutches. Rory's friend Marc Lemieux, who'd found Henry for Sandy, had come in from Montreal to be the best man. The service would be short and meaningful.

The genial, portly pastor of the country church was at the altar, waiting benevolently for the service to begin.

Rory looked very handsome in his new tuxedo, the old one discarded in shreds after the night he spent rescuing Dancer. He was serene as he stood before the altar, and everyone could see that this was the happiest day of his life. Mousie and Rosalyn stood at the back waiting for Christine, while Sandy took a seat beside his grandparents. Joy sat across the aisle with the two dogs hiding under her chair, sure in their scheming doggy minds that no one would notice them. She gave Sandy a conspiratorial wink and pointed them out to him as he seated himself. The church organist began the wedding march from her perch on the patio, where they'd rolled the piano that morning.

All eyes turned toward the house. Christine, whose father had passed away years before, had made the decision that no one else should give her away. To marry Rory was her choice, and her choice alone. She stood tall and proud and happy. She smiled at Rory, a radiant smile that said to all the world that she'd love him until death did them part.

Mousie thought her mother had never looked more beautiful. She wore a flowing mint-green suit, the silk lapelless jacket flaring out below the fitted waist. The flared ankle-length skirt billowed and swayed with every breeze, flattering her long legs. She wore an apricot silk camisole that matched the tiny apricot rhinestone buttons on the sleeves, the four at the front and two at the back of the jacket. Christine carried her fragrant bouquet in mint-green gloved hands, and on her head was a jaunty mint-green cap with a short green veil. She wore her glossy dark hair pulled back into a soft chignon at the nape of her neck. This outfit had been a closely guarded secret, known only to Joy, Christine, and Mousie. There were gasps of approval all around.

Mousie walked up the aisle with grace, to the rhythm of the music. She held her head with pride. As she passed Sandy, she flashed him a special smile, which he returned with enthusiasm.

The guests chuckled, then laughed out loud as Rosalyn made her way up to the altar. She grimaced and wobbled and giggled and finally arrived.

Christine followed. Her eyes were on Rory alone. His eyes were locked on hers. Had the guests not arrived, they would not have noticed.

Mousie sat to the left of the altar, and watched the ceremony, her job done. Her eyes sought out Sandy, who gave her a wink. She looked over to Joy, who smiled at her through happy tears. She scanned the crowd, recognizing relatives and old family friends and people who'd been part of her childhood. Sandy had described some of his more colourful family, and Mousie thought she could pick them out.

Her childhood was over. She was eighteen and ready to take on the world. She had faced difficulties and had overcome them. Her high school graduation would mark the end of an era. Both she and Sandy had been accepted by a number of universities, and the future beckoned.

As she absorbed the people, the event and the day itself, her skin prickled. She felt a presence. She looked to her left. Beside the barn, his chestnut coat shimmering, listening intently to every word, stood Dancer.

Dancer, who'd carried her to victory over countless hurdles. Dancer, who'd been her solace through desperate times. Dancer, strong and valiant and true. And Dancer, who in her mind, was the sometime harbour of her father's spirit.

Was her father with them now, at the wedding? she wondered.

Dancer saw her watching him. He nodded to her. Her heart leapt. He shook his head slightly, mane rippling, keeping her in her seat.

Mousie returned her attention to the wedding in time to see Rory's golden ring slip onto her mother's finger. It was done. Rory gently lifted the veil from Christine's upturned face, caressed her with his eyes, then lovingly, deeply, kissed her. There wasn't a person there who didn't realize the rightness, the goodness of this union.

She turned back to Dancer.

To this day, she isn't sure what she saw. Through eyes blurred with tears, it appeared to her that a vapour rose from Dancer and swirled in a blaze of auburn in the vibrant blue sky overhead. Then it was gone. And she wasn't sure that she'd seen it at all.

Mousie sat momentarily transfixed, the noises right beside her sounding miles away. People all around her rose from their seats and cheered and congratulated Rory and Christine and the party sparkled with fun.

Dancer grazed.

Mousie stumbled over to him and hugged his neck tightly. He bent his front knees and lifted her onto his back with his head. He neighed in his deep echoing stallion tones and reared, thrashing his powerful front legs in the air. He spun around and took off, clearing the three-and-a-half-foot gate from a stand-still. Mousie, bareback and reinless, hung on fiercely, tears of pure joy streaming down her face.

'I love you, Dancer,' she whispered to him.

The stupefied wedding guests watched in awe as the billow of apricot cotton soared over the four-foot stone wall on the other side of the pasture and galloped off into the rolling hills of Caledon.

Glossary of Horse-related Terminology

Bridle: A leather head harness attached to the reins, for controlling the horse.

Check: A rest period during a hunt, at which point the horses and hounds regroup.

Cover: Any wooded area where a fox might hide.

Draw: (Said of hunting hounds) to search an area for a scent.

Dressage: A style of riding in which the horse is taught to perform difficult manoeuvres with no apparent cue being given by the rider.

Field: Riders taking part in a foxhunt. They follow the field-master, who takes directions from the master.

Field master: The hunt official who leads the rest of the people on horses.

Flake of hay: One section of a bale of hay.

Girth: The strap that holds the saddle to the horse.

Hands: The measure of a horse's height from its shoulder to the ground. One hand is equal to four 'fingers', or inches.

Huntsman: The person who trains and manages the hounds.

Line: a) The direction taken by the field (see above) or the hunted animal. b) The breeding or family tree of an animal.

Martingale: The leather strap that connects the saddle to either the bridle or the reins. It enhances control of the horse.

Master: The chief of the hunters. He makes decisions.

Oxer: A square jump consisting of poles.

Riding cap: A safety helmet covered in black velvet.

Saddle: The leather seat fastened on the horse's back.

Scent: The odour of an animal.

Sidesaddle: A saddle fashioned for ladies wearing long skirts, with a hook on one side to support the leg. The ladies did not straddle the horse; both their legs were on the left side of the horse.

Stirrup: The metal foot holder on the saddle, attached by stirrup leathers.

Stock: a) A tie worn with hunting costume. It is fashioned from a long, narrow, piece of white cotton, and doubles as a bandage if the horse is injured. b) Horse *stock* refers to the animals a farmer keeps. c) A horse *stocks up* when he develops swollen ankles.

Sound: The noise a hound makes when he picks up a scent.

Tack: The saddle, bridle, and other parts of the horse's equipment.

Twitch: A thick stick with a loop of rope on the end that encircles the lip of the horse. When the stick is twisted the rope pinches the lip and takes the horse's mind off whatever else is happening. It's usually used when a veterinarian needs to do some work that the horse dislikes.

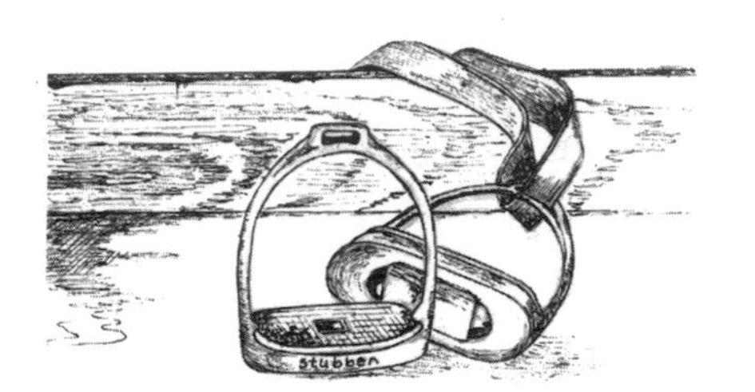
Stubben

Acknowledgements

I THANK my best friend and husband, David, for his unfailing and optimistic support. I thank Ben, Chloë, and Adam for their constant cheerfulness and encouragement.

My mother, Joyce Matthews, was my sounding board. My sisters, Dona, Debbie, Carole Matthews, and Gini Lato refused to let the story remain in my desk drawer. My brother, Jack, was always a phone call away, and my father, Don, taught me that whatever I do, I must do my best. Clarence and Marie Peterson, thank you for showering me with kindness. Tim, Cathy, Jim, Heather – Petersons all – thank you for being family to me.

Marybeth Drake, my dear childhood friend and riding companion, created the beautiful, delicate drawings which adorn these pages so gracefully.

Iris Philips edited my original effort, smoothing the bumps. Nalini Stewart, Marion Doyle, Susan Perren, and Iris Philips gave me the heart to send it again and again to publishers. I thank those same publishers for their constructive criticism, which helped me to write a better book; Jane Somerville in particular.

John Metcalf, with his witty, insightful, and friendly editing, and Doris Cowan's precise, practical pen assisted enormously in polishing the final work.

Thank you Elke and Tim Inkster of the Porcupine's Quill, for believing in *Dancer*, and turning a dream into a reality.

PETER PATERSON

About the Author

SHELLEY PETERSON was born in London, Ontario, the second of six children of Don and Joyce Matthews. She appeared in her first theatrical production, *Pinocchio*, at the Grand Theatre in London at the age of ten. Her professional acting career began with a production of *A Midsummer Night's Dream* at the Neptune Theatre in Halifax when she was nineteen. Since then she has played over a hundred roles on television, in film and on the stage. Youthful viewers will know her as 'Helen' in the YTV television series 'Doghouse'. She was educated at the Banff School of Fine Arts, at Dalhousie and at the University of Western Ontario. Shelley has had a lifelong love for animals big and small – she apparently learned to say 'horsy' before she could say 'mommy'. She has ridden all her life, and has competed in Hunt Night at the Royal Winter Fair.

Shelley currently divides her time between Toronto and Fox Ridge, a horse farm in the Caledon Hills which she shares with her husband, their two sons and daughter, and the family dog, Wile E. Coyote.